EX LIBRIS

The Story of
The Glittering Plain

THE STORY OF THE GLITTERING PLAIN
A BOOK THAT INSPIRED TOLKIEN
- With Original Illustrations -

Book #3 of 'The Professor's Bookshelf'

Cover images by Walter Crane and W.B. MacDougall
Author: Morris, William, 1834-1896 author

Title: The story of the glittering plain : a book that inspired Tolkien
illustrated by William Morris ;
with 23 woodcuts by Walter Crane ;
introduced by Cecilia Dart-Thornton.

ISBN: 9781925110067 (paperback)

Series: The professor's bookshelf ; 3.

Subjects: Fantasy fiction.

Dewey Number: 823.8

Copyright (C) 2018 Leaves of Gold Press
ABN 67 099 575 078
PO Box 3092, Brighton, 3186, Victoria, Australia

The Story of the Glittering Plain

- A Book That Inspired Tolkien -

ACCORDING TO THE 1894 KELMSCOTT EDITION

by William Morris
With 23 Woodcuts by Walter Crane
Introduced by Cecilia Dart-Thornton

and including
THE ART AND CRAFT OF PRINTING
by William Morris

www.professorsbookshelf.com

THE PROFESSOR'S BOOKSHELF

Welcome to The Professor's Bookshelf, a collection of books that inspired the imagination of Professor JRR Tolkien, author of The Hobbit and The Lord of the Rings.

All our titles have informed the professor's writings in one way or another. In most cases the man himself has revealed their influence in his essays or interviews; in others, his biographers and researchers have uncovered the evidence. Some were widely obtainable and popular in his literary circles, so that he certainly knew of them and there is little doubt he read them.

Tolkien's own drawings adorn the pages of The Hobbit and it is easy to imagine him as a boy, long before the invention of television, poring for hours over the images in his favourite volumes - images that helped shape his creation of Middle Earth.

Where possible we have selected illustrated editions available in his lifetime. Both texts and pictures have been reproduced, and our books are mostly copies of the editions the professor held in his own hands.

Like the celebrated nineteenth century English textile designer, artist and writer William Morris, we at The Professor's Bookshelf reject the notion that illustrated materials are unsuitable for adults. To Morris, who was one of Tolkien's favourite authors, illustrated books for adults presented an opportunity to integrate literature with design and art. In essence, a book is itself an artistic creation. The Professor's Bookshelf celebrates this by embellishing our 'Illustrated' series with the original plates (whole page illustrations printed separately from the text), cuts (illustrations printed within the text), borders, fonts, miniatures, and ornamental capital letters, in addition to our own 'endpapers' and bookplates.

Each Professor's Bookshelf classic opens with an introduction by fantasy author Cecilia Dart-Thornton, about whose acclaimed Bitterbynde Trilogy Grand Master of Science Fiction Andre Norton wrote: 'Not since Tolkien's The Lord of the Rings fell into my hands have I been so impressed by a beautifully spun fantasy.'

Literary scholars have studied the texts in The Professor's Bookshelf collection, finding threads and motifs linking them to the professor's famous works. On reading them you will be awakened to that vast library of myth, magic, legend and fantasy whose legacy inspired the great English writer, poet and philologist, J.R.R. Tolkien.

~ SOME TITLES IN THE SERIES ~

1. The Song of the Nibelungs (illustrated)
Translated by Margaret Armour, previously published as 'The Fall of the Nibelungs', illust. W. B. MacDougall, pub. 1897

2. The Poetic Edda (illustrated)
Translated by Olive Bray, previously published as 'The Elder or Poetic Edda', illust. W. G. Collingwood, pub. 1908

3. The Story of the Glittering Plain (illustrated)
By William Morris, illust. Walter Crane, pub.1894

4. The Red Fairy Book (illustrated)
By Andrew Lang, illust. H. J. Ford and Lancelot Speed, pub. 1907

5. The Princess and the Goblin (illustrated)
By George MacDonald, illust. Jessie Willcox Smith, pub. 1920

6. The Saga of Eric Brighteyes (illustrated)
By H. Rider Haggard, illust. Lancelot Speed, pub. 1891.

7. The Dragon Ouroboros (illustrated)
By Eric Rücker Eddison, illust. Keith Henderson, pub. 1922

8. The Book of Wonder & The Last Book of Wonder (illustrated)
By Lord Dunsany, illust. S. H. Syme, pub. 1912

9. The Story of King Arthur and his Knights (illustrated)
Written and illustrated by Howard Pyle, pub. 1903

10. Grimms' Fairytales (illustrated)
Translated by Lucy Crane, illust. Walter Crane, pub. 1922

For more about the The Professor's Bookshelf series, visit
www.professorsbookshelf.com

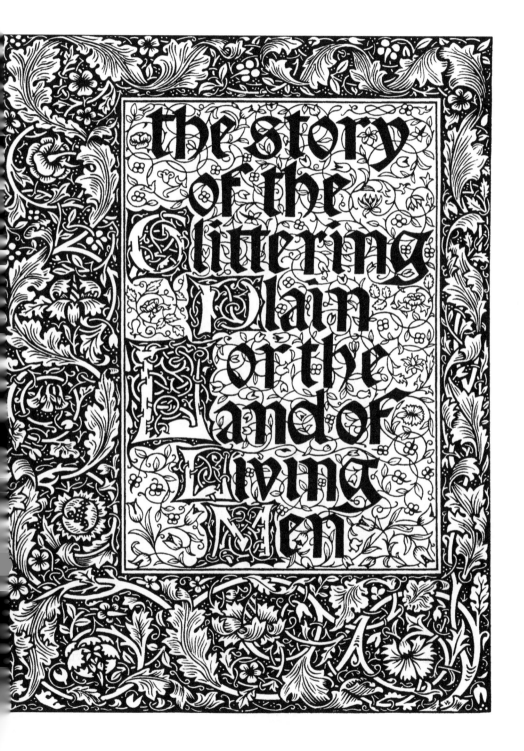

the story of the Glittering Plain or the Land of Living Men

THE STORY OF THE GLITTERING PLAIN WHICH HAS BEEN ALSO
CALLED THE LAND OF LIVING MEN OR THE ACRE OF THE UNDYING.

INTRODUCTION
by Cecilia Dart-Thornton

On May 8, 1891, Kelmscott Press published its first book, *The Story of the Glittering Plain*. This fantasy novel by the famous nineteenth century English textile designer, artist and writer William Morris (1834 – 1896) describes the journey of Hallblithe, a young man on an epic quest to rescue his love.

J.R.R. Tolkien was two years old when the second edition was published in 1894, complete with decorated borders and capitals by Morris and richly detailed illustrations by Walter Crane. This edition is a close copy of that book but also includes Morris's essay collection *The Art and Craft of Printing*.

Fantasy and medieval literature specialist Douglas A. Anderson writes in *Tales Before Tolkien: The Roots of Modern Fantasy*, 'William Morris was an enormous influence on Tolkien in terms of the general shape of his literary interests. Tolkien discovered Morris's translations in his teens, and his interest in Morris deepened at Exeter College, Oxford, where Morris had also been an undergraduate. Tolkien's earliest stories of his Middle Earth legendarium, published posthumously as *The Book of Lost Tales*, show a decided influence of Morris in their archaism and style.'

When Tolkien was twenty-two he revealed, in a letter to his sweetheart Edith, 'Amongst other work I am trying to turn one of the short stories [of the Finnish Kalevala] ... into a short story somewhat on the lines of Morris's romances with chunks of poetry in between.'

In 1960 he was still acknowledging his debt of inspiration to Morris, noting, 'The Lord of the Rings was actually begun, as a separate thing, about 1937, and had reached the inn at Bree, before the shadow of the second war. . . . The Dead Marshes and the approaches to the Morannon owe something to Northern France after the Battle of the Somme. They owe more to William Morris and his Huns and Romans, as in *The House of the Wolfings* or *The Roots of the Mountains*.'

'Morris was perhaps the first modern fantasy writer to unite an imaginary world with the element of the supernatural, and thus the precursor of much of present-day fantasy literature,' wrote L. Sprague de Camp in *Literary Swordsmen and Sorcerers*.

Mary Podles, in her article *Tolkien & the New Art: Visual Sources for The Lord of the Rings*, says, 'We know from Tolkien's letters and various commentaries that [William] Morris's literary works had a profound influence on Tolkien... I hope to demonstrate that certain associates and artistic heirs to Morris did provide visual sources for Tolkien's writing, particularly in their illustrations for the fairy tales that so appealed to him.'

Like Morris, Walter Crane (1845–1915), an English artist and book illustrator, was associated with the Arts and Crafts Movement.
'From the early 1880s, initially under William Morris's influence, Crane did as much as Morris himself to bring art into the daily life of all classes. With this object in view he devoted much attention to designs for textiles and wallpapers, and to house decoration...
'Crane is considered to be the most prolific and influential children's book creator of his generation.' (Wikipedia)

According to Yale University's *The Illustrated Word at the Fin de Siecle* (2006), 'Morris had initially discussed with Walter Crane the possibility of the artist illustrating the 1891 edition of *Glittering Plain*, but Crane's schedule kept him from completing illustrations in a manner timely enough for Morris, who was impatient to get his first book out. It was published with decorated borders and capitals by Morris, but no illustrations. In 1894, *Glittering Plain* became the first and only Kelmscott title to be published twice – this time with 23 woodcut illustrations by Crane. The book was bigger and more elaborate than the first, and, though Crane's illustrations were met with only tepid critical acclaim, the book was popular and well-received.

'Crane was best known for his work as a writer and illustrator of children's books, but Morris rejected the notion that illustrated materials – and, indeed, folk tales and fantasy – were unsuitable for adults. Though avidly interested in children and himself a dedicated father, Morris did not produce materials geared specifically to youngsters. For both Morris and Crane, the 1894 edition of *Glittering Plain* – an illustrated book for adults – was an opportunity to embrace a more integrated philosophy of audience, authorship, and art. They would not show ambivalence toward design just because *Glittering Plain* was meant for older readers; they would celebrate the intrinsically artistic nature of the book by providing illustrations and ornamental capital letters. The edition was a handsome volume available either printed on paper and bound in cloth, or, for some collectors, printed on and bound in vellum. It combined elements of fantasy and legend.

'Its design is a feat of integrated text and image, as well as both collaborators' socialistic artistic philosophies. Crane's illustration, like Morris's text, adopts an idealized, medieval effect, hearkening back to what was commonly thought to be a simpler time. Perhaps symbolic of printers and artisans before the industrial revolution.

'Although the illustration itself [in *The Story of the Glittering Plain*] does not provide explicit commentary on the text, it is essential to the reading of it. [The illustrations are] rich in illustrative detail, incorporating not only naturalistic ornamental elements but also actual letters into all areas of the page – the outer border, the inner border, and the actual text window. Word and image – embodying thought and body, respectively, on the page – are combined in the book's design.'

The Story of the Glittering Plain is one of William Morris's ground-breaking works which helped to inspire JRR Tolkien's creation of *The Hobbit* and *The Lord of the Rings*.

Cecilia Dart-Thornton
Author of The Bitterbynde Trilogy
www.dartthornton.com

for

THE PROFESSOR'S BOOKSHELF

A List of the Chapters of This Book.

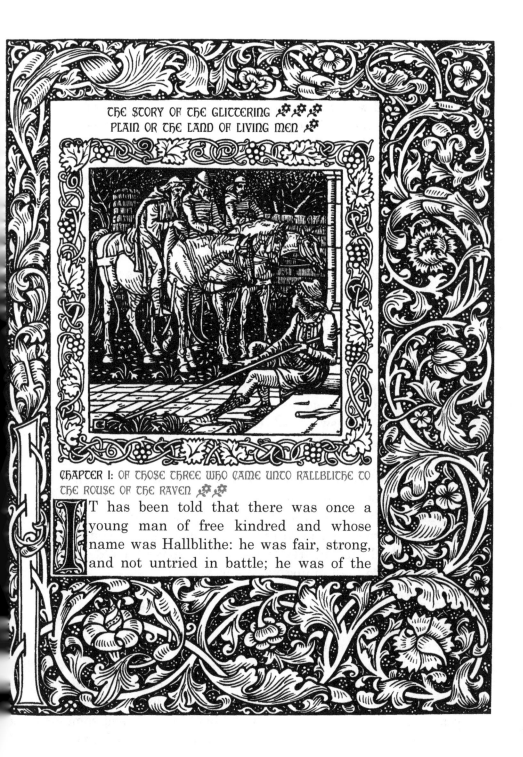

THE STORY OF THE GLITTERING
PLAIN OR THE LAND OF LIVING MEN

CHAPTER I: OF THOSE THREE WHO CAME UNTO HALLBLITHE TO
THE HOUSE OF THE RAVEN

IT has been told that there was once a
young man of free kindred and whose
name was Hallblithe: he was fair, strong,
and not untried in battle; he was of the

House of the Raven of old time 🖉 This man loved an exceeding fair damsel called the Hostage, who was of the House of
the Rose, wherein it was right and due that the men of the
Raven should wed. She loved him no less, and no man of the
kindred gainsaid their love, and they were to be wedded on
Midsummer Night.

BUT one day of early spring, when the days were
yet short & the nights long, Hallblithe sat before
the porch of the house smoothing an ash stave for
his spear, & he heard the sound of horse-hoofs
drawing nigh, and he looked up and saw folk riding toward
the house, and so presently they rode through the garth gate;
and there was no man but he about the house, so he rose up
and went to meet them, and he saw that they were but three
in company: they had weapons with them, and their horses
were of the best; but they were no fellowship for a man to be
afraid of; for two of them were old and feeble, and the third
was dark and sad, and drooping of aspect: it seemed as if
they had ridden far and fast, for their spurs were bloody and
their horses all a-sweat 🖉 Hallblithe hailed them kindly
and said: "Ye are wayworn, and maybe ye have to ride further; so light down and come into the house, and take bite
and sup, and hay and corn also for your horses; and then if
ye needs must ride on your way, depart when ye are rested;
or else if ye may, then abide here night-long, and go your
ways to-morrow, and meantime that which is ours shall be
yours, and all shall be free to you." Then spake the oldest of
the elders in a high piping voice and said:

YOUNG man, we thank thee; but though the days of the
springtide are waxing, the hours of our lives are waning; nor may we abide unless thou canst truly tell us that
this is the Land of the Glittering Plain: and if that be so,
then delay not, lead us to thy lord, and perhaps he will make
us content" 🖉 Spake he who was somewhat less stricken in
years than the first: "Thanks have thou! but we need something more than meat and drink, to wit the Land of Living

Men. And Oh! but the time presses" 🍃 Spake the sad & sorry carle: "We seek the Land where the days are many: so many that he who hath forgotten how to laugh, may learn the craft again, and forget the days of Sorrow."

HEN they all three cried aloud and said: "Is this the Land? Is this the Land?" 🍃 But Hallblithe wondered, and he laughed and said: "Wayfarers, look under the sun down the plain which lieth betwixt the mountains and the sea, and ye shall behold the meadows all gleaming with the spring lilies; yet do we not call this the Glittering Plain, but Cleveland by the Sea. Here men die when their hour comes, nor know I if the days of their life be long enough for the forgetting of sorrow; for I am young and not yet a yokefellow of sorrow; but this I know, that they are long enough for the doing of deeds that shall not die. And as for Lord, I know not this word, for here dwell we, the sons of the Raven, in good fellowship, with our wives that we have wedded, and our mothers who have borne us, and our sisters who serve us. Again I bid you light down off your horses, and eat and drink, and be merry; & depart when ye will, to seek what land ye will" 🍃 They scarce looked on him, but cried out together mournfully: "This is not the Land! This is not the Land!" 🍃 No more than that they said, but turned about their horses and rode out through the garth gate, & went clattering up the road that led to the pass of the mountains. But Hallblithe hearkened wondering, till the sound of their horse-hoofs died away, & then turned back to his work: and it was then two hours after high-noon.

CHAPTER II: EVIL TIDINGS COME TO HAND AT CLEVELAND

OT long had he worked ere he heard the sound of horse-hoofs once more, and he looked not up, but said to himself, "It is but the lads bringing back the teams from the acres, and riding fast and driving hard for joy of heart and in wantonness of youth" But the sound grew nearer and he looked up and saw over the turf wall of the garth the flutter of white raiment; and he said: "Nay, it is the maidens coming back from the

sea-shore and the gathering of wrack" 🪶 So he set himself
the harder to his work, and laughed, all alone as he was, and
said: "She is with them: now I will not look up again till they
have ridden into the garth, and she has come from among
them, and leapt off her horse and cast her arms about my
neck as her wont is; & it will rejoice her then to mock me
with hard words and kind voice and longing heart; and I
shall long for her and kiss her, and sweet shall the coming
days seem to us: and the daughters of our folk shall look on
and be kind and blithe with us" 🪶 Therewith rode the maidens into the garth, but he heard no sound of laughter or
merriment amongst them, which was contrary to their wont;
and his heart fell, and it was as if instead of the maidens'
laughter the voices of those wayfarers came back upon the
wind crying out, "Is this the Land? Is this the Land?" 🪶
Then he looked up hastily, and saw the maidens drawing
near, ten of the House of the Raven, and three of the House
of the Rose; and he beheld them that their faces were pale
and woe-begone, and their raiment rent, and there was no
joy in them. Hallblithe stood aghast while one who had gotten off her horse (and she was the daughter of his own
mother) ran past him into the hall, looking not at him, as if
she durst not: & another rode off swiftly to the horse-stalls.
But the others, leaving their horses, drew round about him,
and for a while none durst utter a word; and he stood gazing
at them, with the spoke-shave in his hand, he also silent; for
he saw that the Hostage was not with them, and he knew
that now he was the yokefellow of sorrow 🪶 At last he spoke
gently and in a kind voice, and said: "Tell me, sisters, what
evil hath befallen us, even if it be the death of a dear friend,
& the thing that may not be amended" 🪶 Then spoke a fair
woman of the Rose, whose name was Brightling, and said:
"Hallblithe, it is not of death that we have to tell, but of sundering, which may yet be amended. We were on the sand of
the sea nigh the Ship-stead and the Rollers of the Raven,
and we were gathering the wrack & playing together; & we
saw a round-ship nigh to shore lying with her sheet slack,
and her sail beating the mast; but we deemed it to be none

other than some bark of the Fish-biters, and thought no harm thereof, but went on running and playing amidst the little waves that fell on the sand, and the ripples that curled around our feet. At last there came a small boat from the side of the round-ship, and rowed in toward shore, and still we feared not, though we drew a little aback from the surf and let fall our gown-hems. But the crew of that boat beached her close to where we stood, and came hastily wading the surf toward us; & we saw that they were twelve weaponed men, great, and grim, & all clad in black raiment. Then indeed were we afraid, and we turned about and fled up the beach; but now it was too late, for the tide was at more than half ebb and long was the way over the sand to the place where we had left our horses tied among the tamarisk-bushes. Nevertheless we ran, & had gotten up to the pebble-beach before they ran in amongst us: and they caught us, and cast us down on to the hard stones 🖋 Then they made us sit in a row on a ridge of the pebbles; and we were sore afraid, yet more for defilement at their hands than for death; for they were evil-looking men exceeding foul of favour. Then said one of them: 'Which of all you maidens is the Hostage of the House of the Rose?' Then all we kept silence, for we would not betray her. But the evil man spake again: 'Choose ye then whether we shall take one, or all of you across the waters in our black ship.' Yet still we others spake not, till arose thy beloved, O Hallblithe, and said: 'Let it be one then, and not all; for I am the Hostage.' 'How shalt thou make us sure thereof?' said the evil carle. She looked on him proudly & said: 'Because I say it.' 'Wilt thou swear it?' said he. 'Yea,' said she, 'I swear it by the token of the House wherein I shall wed; by the wings of the Fowl that seeketh the Field of Slaying.' 'It is enough,' said the man, 'come thou with us. And ye maidens sit ye there, and move not till we have made way on our ship, unless ye would feel the point of the arrow. For ye are within bow-shot of the ship, and we have shot-weapons aboard.' So the Hostage departed with them, & she unweeping, but we wept sorely. And we saw the small boat come up to the side of the round-ship, and the

Hostage going over the gunwale along with those evil men, and we heard the hale and how of the mariners as they drew up the anchor and sheeted home; and then the sweeps came out and the ship began to move over the sea. And one of those evil-minded men bent his bow and shot a shaft at us, but it fell far short of where we sat, and the laugh of those runagates came over the sands to us. So we crept up the beach trembling, and then rose to our feet & got to our horses, and rode hither speedily, and our hearts are broken for thy sorrow."

AT that word came Hallblithe's own sister out from the hall; and she bore weapons with her, to wit Hallblithe's sword and shield and helm and hauberk. 🖉 As for him he turned back silently to his work, and set the steel of the spear on the new ashen shaft, & took the hammer and smote the nail in, and laid the weapon on a round pebble that was thereby, and clenched the nail on the other side. Then he looked about, and saw that the other damsel had brought him his coal-black warhorse ready saddled and bridled; then he did on his armour, and girt his sword to his side and leapt into the saddle, and took his new-shafted spear in hand & shook the rein. But none of all those damsels durst say a word to him or ask him whither he went, for they feared his face, & the sorrow of his heart. So he got him out of the garth and turned toward the sea-shore, and they saw the glitter of his spear-point a minute over the turf-wall, and heard the clatter of his horse-hoofs as he galloped over the hard way; and thus he departed.

CHAPTER III: THE WARRIORS OF THE RAVEN SEARCH THE SEAS

HEN the women bethought them, and they spake a word or two together, & then they sundered and went one this way and one that, to gather together the warriors of the Raven who were a-field, or on the way, nigh unto the house, that they might follow Hallblithe down to the sea-shore and help him; after a while they came back again by one and two

and three, bringing with them the wrathful young men; and
when there was upward of a score gathered in the garth
armed and horsed, they rode their ways to the sea, being
minded to thrust a long-ship of the Ravens out over the Rollers into the sea, and follow the strong-thieves of the waters
and bring a-back the Hostage, so that they might end the
sorrow at once, & establish joy once more in the House of the
Raven & the House of the Rose. But they had with them
three lads of fifteen winters or thereabouts to lead their
horses back home again, when they should have gone up on
to the Horse of the Brine.

THUS then they departed, and the maidens stood in the
garth-gate till they lost sight of them behind the sandhills, & then turned back sorrowfully into the house, and sat
there talking low of their sorrow. And many a time they had
to tell their tale anew, as folk came into the hall one after
another from field and fell. But the young men came down
to the sea, and found Hallblithe's black horse straying about
amongst the tamarisk-bushes above the beach; & they looked
thence over the sand, and saw neither Hallblithe nor any
man: and they gazed out seaward, and saw neither ship nor
sail on the barren brine. Then they went down on to the sand,
and sundered their fellowship, and went half one way, half
the other, betwixt the sandhills and the surf, where now the
tide was flowing, till the nesses of the east and the west, the
horns of the bay, stayed them. Then they met together again
by the Rollers, when the sun was within an hour of setting.
There and then they laid hand to that ship which is called
the Seamew, and they ran her down over the Rollers into the
waves, & leapt aboard and hoisted sail, and ran out the oars
and put to sea; & a little wind was blowing seaward from the
gates of the mountains behind them ✦ So they quartered
the sea-plain, as the kestrel doth the water-meadows, till the
night fell on them, and was cloudy, though whiles the waning
moon shone out; and they had seen nothing, neither sail nor
ship, nor aught else on the barren brine, save the washing
of waves and the hovering of sea-fowl. So they lay-to outside

the horns of the bay and awaited the dawning. And when morning was come they made way again, and searched the sea, and sailed to the out-skerries, and searched them with care; then they sailed into the main and fared hither and thither and up & down: and this they did for eight days, and in all that time they saw no ship nor sail, save three barks of the Fish-biters nigh to the Skerry which is called Mew-stone 🍃 So they fared home to the Raven Bay, and laid their keel on the Rollers, and so went their ways sadly, home to the House of the Raven: and they deemed that for this time they could do no more in seeking their valiant kinsman and his fair damsel. And they were very sorry; for these two were well-beloved of all men. But since they might not amend it, they abode in peace, awaiting what the change of days might bring them.

CHAPTER IV: NOW HALLBLITHE TAKETH THE SEA

OW must it be told of Hallblithe that he rode fiercely down to the sea shore, & from the top of the beach he gazed about him, & there below him was the Shipstead and Rollers of his kindred, whereon lay the three long-ships, the Seamew, & the Osprey and the Erne. Heavy and huge they seemed to him as they lay there, black-sided, icy-cold with the washing of the March waves,

their golden dragon-heads looking seaward wistfully. But
first had he peered out into the offing, and it was only when
he had let his eyes come back from where the sea and sky
met, and they had beheld nothing but the waste of waters,
that he beheld the Ship-stead closely; and therewith he saw
where a little to the west of it lay a skiff, which the low wave
of the tide lifted and let fall from time to time. It had a mast,
and a black sail hoisted thereon and flapping with slackened
sheet. A man sat in the boat clad in black raiment, & the sun
smote a gleam from the helm on his head 🖋 Then Hallblithe leapt off his horse, and strode down the sands
shouldering his spear; and when he came near to the man in
the boat he poised his spear and shook it and cried out: "Man,
art thou friend or foe?" 🖋 Said the man: "Thou art a fair
young man: but there is grief in thy voice along with wrath
🖋 Cast not till thou hast heard me, and mayst deem whether
I may do aught to heal thy grief' 🖋 "What mayst thou do?"
said Hallblithe; "art thou not a robber of the sea, a harrier of
the folks that dwell in peace?"

HE man laughed: "Yea," said he, "my craft is thieving
and carrying off the daughters of folk, so that we may
have a ransom for them. Wilt thou come over the waters
with me?" 🖋 Hallblithe said wrathfully: "Nay, rather, come
thou ashore here! Thou seemest a big man, & belike shalt be
good of thine hands. Come and fight with me; & then he of
us who is vanquished, if he be unslain, shall serve the other
for a year, and then shalt thou do my business in the ran-
soming" 🖋 The man in the boat laughed again, and that so
scornfully that he angered Hallblithe beyond measure: then
he arose in the boat and stood on his feet swaying from side
to side as he laughed. He was passing big, long-armed &
big-headed, and long hair came from under his helm like the
tail of a red horse; his eyes were grey and gleaming, and his
mouth wide.

IN a while he stayed his laughter and said: "O Warrior of the Raven, this were a simple game for thee to play; though it is not far from my mind, for fighting when I needs must win is no dull work. Look you, if I slay or vanquish thee, then all is said; and if by some chance stroke thou slayest me, then is thine only helper in this matter gone from thee. Now to be short, I bid thee come aboard to me if thou wouldst ever hear another word of thy damsel betrothed. And moreover this need not hinder thee to fight with me if thou have a mind to it thereafter; for we shall soon come to a land big enough for two to stand on. Or if thou listest to fight in a boat rocking on the waves, I see not but there may be manhood in that also."

NOW was the hot wrath somewhat run off Hallblithe, nor durst he lose any chance to hear a word of his beloved; so he said: "Big man, I will come aboard. But look thou to it, if thou hast a mind to bewray me; for the sons of the Raven die hard" 🖋 "Well," said the big man, "I have heard that their minstrels are of many words, and think that they have tales to tell. Come aboard and loiter not." Then Hallblithe waded the surf & lightly strode over the gunwale of the skiff and sat him down. The big man thrust out into the deep and haled home the sheet; but there was but little wind 🖋 Then said Hallblithe: "Wilt thou have me row, for I wot not whitherward to steer?" 🖋 Said the red carle: "Maybe thou art not in a hurry; I am not: do as thou wilt." So Hallblithe took the oars and rowed mightily, while the alien steered, & they went swiftly and lightly over the sea, and the waves were little.

CHAPTER V: THEY COME UNTO THE ISLE OF RANSOM

S O the sun grew low, and it set; the stars and the moon shone a while and then it clouded over. Hallblithe still rowed and rested not, though he was weary; and the big man sat and steered, and held his peace. But when the night was grown old and it was not far from the dawn, the alien said: "Youngling of the Ravens, now shalt thou sleep and I will row." Hallblithe was exceeding weary; so he gave the oars to the alien and lay down in the stern and slept.

AND in his sleep he dreamed that he was lying in the House of the Raven, and his sisters came to him and said, "Rise up now, Hallblithe! wilt thou be a sluggard on the day of thy wedding? Come thou with us to the House of the Rose that we may bear away the Hostage" Then he dreamed that they departed, and he arose and clad himself: but when he would have gone out of the hall, then was it no longer daylight, but moonlight, and he dreamed that he had dreamed: nevertheless he would have gone abroad, but might not find the door; so he said he would go out by a window; but the wall was high and smooth (quite other than in the House of the Raven, where were low windows all along one aisle), nor was there any way to come at them. But he dreamed that he was so abashed thereat, and had such a weakness on him, that he wept for pity of himself: and he went to his bed to lie down; and lo! there was no bed and no hall; nought but a heath, wild & wide, and empty under the moon. And still he wept in his dream, and his manhood seemed departed from him, and he heard a voice crying out, "Is this the Land? Is this the Land?"

THEREWITHAL he awoke, & as his eyes cleared he beheld the big man rowing and the black sail flapping against the mast; for the wind had fallen dead and they were faring on over a long smooth swell of the sea. It was broad daylight, but round about them was a thick mist, which seemed none the less as if the sun were ready to shine through it As Hallblithe caught the red man's eye, he smiled and nodded on him and said: "Now has the time come for thee first to eat and then to row. But tell me what is that upon thy cheeks?" Hallblithe, reddening somewhat, said: "The night dew hath fallen on me" Quoth the sea-rover, "It is no shame for thee a youngling to remember thy betrothed in thy sleep, and to weep because thou lackest her. But now bestir thee, for it is later than thou mayest deem" Therewith the big man drew in the oars and came to the after-part of the boat, and drew meat & drink out of a locker thereby; and they ate & drank together,

& Hallblithe grew strong and somewhat less downcast; and he went forward and gat the oars into his hands 🗦 Then the big red man stood up and looked over his left shoulder and said: "Soon shall we have a breeze and bright weather" 🗦 Then he looked into the midmost of the sail and fell a-whistling such a tune as the fiddles play to dancing men and maids at Yule-tide, and his eyes gleamed and glittered therewithal, and exceeding big he looked 🗦 Then Hallblithe felt a little air on his cheek, and the mist grew thinner, and the sail began to fill with wind till the sheet tightened: then, lo! the mist rising from the face of the sea, and the sea's face rippling gaily under a bright sun. Then the wind increased, and the wall of mist departed and a few light clouds sped over the sky, & the sail swelled and the boat heeled over, & the seas fell white from the prow, and they sped fast over the face of the waters 🗦 Then laughed the red-haired man, & said: "O croaker on the dead branch, now is the wind such that no rowing of thine may catch up with it: so in with the oars now, & turn about, and thou shalt see whitherward we are going."

HEN Hallblithe turned about on the thwart and looked across the sea, and lo! before them the high cliffs & crags and mountains of a new land which seemed to be an isle, & they were deep blue under the sun, which now shone aloft in the mid heaven. He said nought at all, but sat looking and wondering what land it might be; but the big man said: "O tomb of warriors, is it not as if the blueness of the deep sea had heaved itself up aloft, and turned from coloured air into rock and stone, so wondrous blue it is? But that is because those crags and mountains are so far away, and as we draw nigher to them, thou shalt see them as they verily are, that they are coal-black; and yonder land is an isle, and is called the Isle of Ransom. Therein shall be the market for thee where thou mayst cheapen thy betrothed. There mayst thou take her by the hand and lead her away thence, when thou hast dealt with the chapman of maidens & hast pledged thee by the fowl of battle, & the edge of the fallow blade to pay that which he will have of thee."

AS the big man spoke there was a mocking in his voice and his face and in his whole huge body, which made the sword of Hallblithe uneasy in his scabbard; but he refrained his wrath, and said: "Big man, the longer I look, the less I can think how we are to come up on to yonder island; for I can see nought but a huge cliff, & great mountains rising beyond it" *"Thou shalt the more wonder," said the alien, "the nigher thou drawest thereto; for it is not because we are far away that thou canst see no beach or strand, or sloping of the land seaward, but because there is nought of all these things. Yet fear not! am I not with thee? thou shalt come ashore on the Isle of Ransom" *Then Hallblithe held his peace, and the other spake not for a while, but gave a short laugh once or twice; & said at last in a big voice, "Little Carrion-biter, why dost thou not ask me of my name?" *Now Hallblithe was a tall man and a fell fighter; but he said: "Because I was thinking of other things and not of thee" *"Well," said the big man, in a voice still louder, "when I am at home men call me the Puny Fox." Then Hallblithe said: "Art thou a Fox? It may well be that thou shalt beguile me, as such beasts will; but look to it, that if thou dost I shall know how to avenge me" *Then rose up the big man from the helm, and straddled wide in the boat, and cried out in a great roaring voice: "Crag-nester, I am one of seven brethren, and the smallest and weakest of them. Art thou not afraid?" "No," said Hallblithe, "for the six others are not here. Wilt thou fight here in boat, O Fox?" "Nay," said Fox, "rather we will drink a cup of wine together."

SO he opened the locker again & drew out thence a great horn of some huge neat of the outlands, which was girthed and stopped with silver, and also a golden cup, and he filled the cup from the horn and gave it into Hallblithe's hand and said: "Drink, O

black-fledged nestling! But call a health over the cup if thou
wilt." So Hallblithe raised the cup aloft and cried: "Health to
the House of the Raven and to them that love it! an ill day to
its foemen!" Then he set his lips to the cup and drank; and
that wine seemed to him better and stronger than any he
had ever tasted. But when he had given the cup back again
to Fox, that red one filled it again, and cried over it, "The
Treasure of the Sea! & the King that dieth not!" Then he
drank, and filled again for Hallblithe, and steered with his
knees meanwhile; and thus they drank three cups each, and
Fox smiled and was peaceful and said but little, but Hallblithe sat wondering how the world was changed for him since
yesterday.

BUT now was the sky blown all clear of clouds
and the wind piped shrill behind them, & the
great waves rose & fell about them, & the sun
glittered on them in many colours. Fast flew the
boat before the wind as though it would never stop, and
the day was waning, and the wind still rising; and now the
Isle of Ransom uphove huge before them, and coal-black,
& no beach and no haven was to be seen therein; and still
they ran before the wind towards that black cliff-wall,
against which the sea washed for ever, and no keel ever
built by man might live for one moment 'twixt the surf and
the cliff of that grim land. The sun grew low, and sank red
under the sea, and that world of stone swallowed up half
the heavens before them, for they were now come very nigh
thereto; nor could Hallblithe see aught for it, but that they
must be dashed against the cliff and perish in a moment of
time ✒ Still the boat flew on; but now when the twilight
was come, and they had just opened up along reach of the
cliff that lay beyond a high ness, Hallblithe thought he saw
down by the edge of the sea something darker than the
face of the rock-wall, and he deemed it was a cave: they
came a little nearer and he saw it was a great cave high
enough to let a round-ship go in with all her sails set.

"SON of the Raven," quoth Fox, "hearken, for thy heart is not little. Yonder is the gate into the Isle of Ransom, & if thou wilt, thou mayst go through it. Yet it may be that if thou goest ashore on to the Isle something grievous shall befall thee, a trouble more than thou canst bear: a shame it may be. Now there are two choices for thee: either to go up on to the Isle and face all; or to die here by my hand having done nothing unmanly or shameful: What sayest thou?" "Thou art of many words when time so presses, Fox," said Hallblithe. "Why should I not choose to go up on to the Island to deliver my trothplight maiden? For the rest, slay me if thou canst, if we come alive out of this cauldron of waters" Said the big red man: "Look on then, and note Fox how he steereth, as it were through a needle's eye."

NOW were they underneath the black shadow of the black cliff, and amidst the twilight the surf was tossed about like white fire In the lower heavens the stars were beginning to twinkle & the moon was bright and yellow, and aloft all was peaceful, for no cloud sullied the sky. One moment Hallblithe saw all this hanging above the turmoil of thundering water and dripping rock and the next he was in the darkness of the cave, the roaring wind and the waves still making thunder about him, though of a different voice from the harsh hubbub without. Then he heard Fox say: "Sit down now & take the oars, for presently shall we be at home at the landing place" So Hallblithe took the oars and rowed, and as they went up the cave the sea fell, and the wind died out into the aimless gustiness of hollow places; & for a little while was all as dark as dark might be. Then Hallblithe saw that the darkness grew a little greyer, and he looked over his shoulder and saw a star of light before the bows of the boat, and Fox cried out: "Yea, it is like day; bright will the moon be for such as needs must be wayfaring to-night! Cease rowing, O Son of the coal-blue fowl, for there is way enough on her."

HEN Hallblithe lay on his oars, and in a minute the bows smote the land; then he turned about and saw a steep stair of stone, and up the sloping shaft thereof the moonlit sky and the bright stars *✿* Then Fox arose and came forward and leapt out of the boat and moored her to a big stone: then he leapt back again and said: "Bear a hand with the victuals; we must bring them out of the boat unless thou wilt sleep supperless, as I will not. For to-night must we be guests to ourselves, since it is far to the dwelling of my people, and the old man is said to be a skin-changer, a flit-by-night. And as to this cave, it is deemed to be nowise safe to sleep therein, unless the sleeper have a double share of luck *✿* And thy luck, meseemeth, O Son of the Raven, is as now somewhat less than a single share. So to-night we shall sleep under the naked heaven" *✿* Hallblithe yea-said this, and they took the meat and drink, such as they needed, from out the boat, and climbed the steep stair no little way, & so came out on to a plain place, which seemed to Hallblithe bare & waste so far as he saw it by the moonlight; for the twilight was gone now, and nought was left of the light of day save a glimmer in the west *✿* This Hallblithe deemed wonderful, that no less out on the open heath and brow of the land than in the shut-in cave, all that tumult of the wind had fallen, and the cloudless night was calm, and with a lit-tle air blowing from the south and the landward.

HEREWITHAL was Fox done with his loud-voiced braggart mood, and spoke gently and peaceably like to a wayfarer, who hath business of his to look to as other men. Now he pointed to certain rocks or low crags that a little way off rose like a reef out of the treeless plain; then said he: "Shipmate, underneath yonder rocks is our resting-place for to-night; and I pray thee not to deem me churlish that I give thee no better harbour. But I have a charge over thee to bring thee safe thus far on thy quest; and thou wouldst find it hard to live amongst such house-mates as thou wouldst find up yonder amongst our folks to-night *✿* But to-morrow shalt thou come to speech with him who will deal with thee concerning the ransom" 🍃 "It is enough," said Hallblithe, "& I thank thee for thy leading: and as for thy rough and uncomely words which thou hast given me, I pardon thee for them: for I am none the worse of them: forsooth, if I had been, my sword would have had a voice in the matter" 🍃 "I am well content as it is, Son of the Raven," quoth Fox; "I have done my bidding & all is well" 🍃 Said Hallblithe: "Tell me then who it is hath bidden thee bring me hither?" "I may not tell thee," said Fox; "thou art here, be content, as I am." And he spake no more till they had come to the reef aforesaid, which was some two furlongs from the place where they had come from out of the cave. There then they set forth their supper on the stones, and ate what they would, & drank of that good strong wine while the horn bare out. And now was Fox of few words, & when Hallblithe asked him concerning that land, he had little to say. And at last when Hallblithe asked him of that so perilous house and those who manned it, he said to him: "Son of the Raven, it avails not asking of these matters; for if I tell thee aught concerning them I shall tell thee lies. Once again let it be enough for thee that thou hast passed over the sea safely on thy quest; and a more perilous sea it is forsooth than thou deemest. But now let us have an end of vain words, and make our bed amidst these stones as best we may; for we should be stirring betimes in the morning." Hallblithe said little in answer, & they arrayed their sleeping places cunningly, as the hare doth her form, and like men well used to lying abroad.

HALLBLITHE was very weary and he soon fell asleep; and as he lay there, he dreamed a dream, or maybe saw a vision; whether he were asleep when he saw it, or between sleeping & waking, I know not. But this was his dream or his vision; that the Hostage was standing over him, and she as he had seen her but yesterday, bright-haired and ruddy-cheeked and white-skinned, kind of hand & soft of voice, and she said to him: "Hallblithe, look on me and hearken, for I have a message for thee." And he looked and longed for her, and his soul was ravished by the sweetness of his longing, and he would have leapt up and cast his arms about her, but sleep and the dream bound him, & he might not. Then the image smiled on him and said: "Nay, my love, lie still, for thou mayst not touch me: here is but the image of the body which thou desirest. Hearken then. I am in evil plight, in the hands of strong-thieves of the sea, nor know I what they will do with me, and I have no will to be shamed; to be sold for a price from one hand to another, yet to be bedded without a price, & to lie beside some foeman of our folk, and he to cast his arms about me, will I, will I not: this is a hard case. Therefore to-morrow morning at daybreak while men sleep, I think to steal forth to the gunwale of the black ship & give myself to the gods, that they and not these runagates may be masters of my life and my soul, and may do with me as they will: for indeed they know that I may not bear the strange kinless house, & the love and caressing of the alien house-master, and the mocking and stripes of the alien house-mistress. Therefore let the Hoary One of the sea take me and look to my matters, and carry me to life or death, which-so he will. Thin now grows the night, but be still a little yet, while I speak another word. "Maybe we shall meet alive again, and maybe not: & if not, though we have never yet lain in one bed together, yet I would have thee remember me: yet not so that my image shall come between thee and thy speech-friend and bed-fellow of the kindred, that shall lie where I was to have lain. Yet again, if I live and thou livest, I have been told and have heard that by one way or other I am like to come to the Glittering Plain, & the Land of Living Men. O my beloved, if by any way thou mightest come thither also, & we might meet there, & we two alive, how good it were! Seek that land then, beloved! seek it, whether or no we once more behold the House of the Rose, or tread the floor of the Raven dwelling. And now must even this image of me sunder from thee. Farewell!"

HEREWITH was the dream done and the vision departed; and Hallblithe sat up full of anguish and longing; & he looked about him over the dreary land, & it was somewhat light & the sky was grown grey and cloudy, and he deemed that the dawn was come. So he leapt to his feet & stooped down over Fox, and took him by the shoulder, and shook him and said: "Faring-fellow, awake! the dawn is come, and we have much to do" 🍂 Fox sat up and growled like a dog, & rubbed his eyes and looked about him and said: "Thou hast waked me for nought: it is the false dawn of the moon that shineth now behind the clouds and casteth no shadow; it is but an hour after midnight. Go to sleep again, and let me be, else will I not be a guide to thee when the day comes." And he lay down and was asleep at once. Then Hallblithe went and lay down again full of sorrow: Yet so weary was he that he presently fell asleep, & dreamed no more.

CHAPTER VI: OF A DWELLING OF MAN ON THE ISLE OF RANSOM 🌸🌸

WHEN he awoke again the sun shone on him, and the morning was calm & windless. He sat up and looked about him, but could see no signs of Fox save the lair wherein he had lain. So he arose to his feet and sought for him about the crannies of the rocks, and found him not; & he shouted for him, and had no answer. Then he said, "Belike he has gone down to the boat to put a thing in, or take a thing out." So he went his ways to the

stair down into the water-cave, and he called on Fox from
the top of the stair, and had no answer.

SO he went down that long stair with a misgiving in his
heart, and when he came to the last step there was neither man nor boat, nor aught else save the water and the
living rock. Then was he exceeding wroth, for he knew that
he had been beguiled, and he was in an evil case, left alone
on an Isle that he knew not, a waste & desolate land, where
it seemed most like he should die of famine 🍃 He wasted no
breath or might now in crying out for Fox, or seeking him;
for he said to himself: "I might well have known that he was
false & a liar, whereas he could scarce refrain his joy at my
folly and his guile. Now is it for me to strive for life against
death" 🍃 Then he turned and went slowly up the stair, and
came out on to the open face of that Isle, and he saw that it
was waste indeed, and dreadful: a wilderness of black sand
and stones and ice-borne rocks, with here and there a little
grass growing in the hollows, and here and there a dreary
mire where the white-tufted rushes shook in the wind, and
here and there stretches of moss blended with red-blossomed
sengreen; and otherwhere nought but the wind-bitten creeping willow clinging to the black sand, with a white bleached
stick and a leaf or two, and again a stick and a leaf. In the
offing looking landward were great mountains, some very
great & snow-capped, some bare to the tops; and all that was
far away, save the snow, was deep-blue in the sunny morning. But about him on the heath were scattered rocks like
the reef beneath which he had slept the last night, and
peaks, and hammers, and knolls of uncouth shapes 🍃 Then
he went to the edge of the cliffs and looked down on the sea
which lay wrinkled and rippling on toward the shore far
below him, and long he gazed thereon and all about, but
could see neither ship nor sail, nor aught else save the washing of waves and the hovering of sea fowl 🍃 Then he said:
"Were it not well if I were to seek that house-master of whom
Fox spake? Might he not flit me at least to the Land of the
Glittering Plain? Woe is me! now am I of that woful

company, and I also must needs cry out, Where is the land? Where is the land?"

HEREWITH he turned toward the reef above their lair, but as he went, he thought and said: "Nay, but was not this Stead a lie like the rest of Fox's tale? and am I not alone in this sea-girt wilderness? Yea, and even that image of my Beloved which I saw in the dream, perchance that also was a mere beguiling; for now I see that the Puny Fox was in all ways wiser than is meet and comely." Yet again he said: "At least I will seek on, and find out whether there be another man dwelling on this hapless Isle, and then the worst of it will be battle with him, and death by point and edge rather than by hunger; or at the best we may become friends and fellows and deliver each other." Therewith he came to the reef, and with much ado climbed to the topmost of its rocks and looked down thence landward: and betwixt him and the mountains, and by seeming not very far off, he saw smoke arising: but no house he saw, nor any other token of a dwelling. So he came down from the stone & turned his back upon the sea and went toward that smoke with his sword in its sheath, and his spear over his shoulder. Rough & toilsome was the way: three little dales he crossed amidst the mountain necks, each one narrow and bare, with a stream of water amidst, running seaward, and whether in dale or on ridge, he went ever amidst sand and stones, and the weeds of the wilderness, and saw no man, or man-tended beast.

T last, after he had been four hours on the way, but had not gone very far, he topped a stony bent, and from the brow thereof beheld a wide valley grass-grown for the more part, with a river running through it, and sheep and kine and horses feeding up and down it. And amidst this dale by the stream-side, was a dwelling of men, a long hall, and other houses about it builded of stone Then was Hallblithe glad, and he strode down the bent speedily, his war-gear clashing upon him: and as he came to the foot thereof and on to the grass of the dale, he got amongst the pasturing horses, and passed close by the horse-herd and a woman that was with him. They scowled at him as he went by, but meddled not with him in any way. Although they were giant-like of stature & fierce of face, they were not ill-favoured: they were red-haired, and the woman as white as cream where the sun had not burned her skin; they had no weapons that Hallblithe might see save the goad in the hand of the carle.

SO Hallblithe passed on and came to the biggest house, the hall aforesaid: it was very long, & low as for its length, not over shapely of fashion, a mere gabled heap of stones. Low & strait was the door thereinto, & as Hallblithe entered, stooping lowly, and the fire of the steel of his spear that he held before him was quenched in the mirk of the hall, he smiled and said to himself: "Now if there were one anigh who would not have me enter alive, and he with a weapon in his hand, soon were all the tale told." But he got into the hall unsmitten, and stood on the floor thereof, and spake: "The sele of the day to whomsoever is herein! Will any man speak to the new comer?"

BUT none answered or gave him greeting; and as his eyes got used to the dusk of the hall, he looked about him, & neither on the floor or the high seat nor in any ingle could he see a man; and there was silence there, save for the crackling of the flickering flame on the hearth amidmost, and the running of the rats behind the panelling of the walls 🌿 On one side of the hall was a row of shut-beds, & Hallblithe deemed that there might be men therein; but since none had greeted him, herefrained him from searching them for fear of a trap, and he thought: "I will abide amidst the floor, and if there be any that would deal with me, friend or foe, let him come hither to me."

SO he fell to walking up and down the hall from buttery to dais, & his war-gear rattled upon him. At last as he walked he thought he heard a small thin peevish voice, which yet was too husky for the squeak of a rat. So he stayed his walk and stood still, and said: "Will any man speak to Hallblithe, a new-comer, & a stranger in this Stead?" 🖋 Then that small voice made a word and said: "Why paceth the fool up and down our hall, doing nothing, even as the Ravens flap croaking about the crags, abiding the war-mote and the clash of the fallow blades?" 🖋 Said Hallblithe, and his voice sounded big in the hall: "Who calleth Hallblithe a fool and mocketh at the sons of the Raven?" 🖋 Spake the voice: "Why cometh not the fool to the man that may not go to him?" 🖋 Then Hallblithe bent forward to hearken, and he deemed that the voice came from one of the shut-beds, so he leaned his spear against a pillar, and went into the shut-bed he had noted, & saw where there lay along in it a man exceeding old by seeming, sore wasted, with long hair as white as snow lying over the bed-clothes.

WHEN the elder saw Hallblithe, he laughed a thin cracked laugh as if in mockery and said: "Hail new-comer! wilt thou eat?" "Yea," said Hallblithe 🖋 "Go thou into the buttery then," said the old carle, "and there shalt thou find on the cupboard cakes, & curds and cheese: eat thy fill, and when thou hast done, look in the ingle, and thou shalt see a cask of mead exceeding good, and a stoup thereby, and two silver cups; fill the stoup and bring it hither with the cups; and then may we talk amidst of drinking, which is good for an old carle. Hasten thou! or I shall deem thee a double fool who will not fare to fetch his meat, though he be hungry" 🖋 Then Hallblithe laughed, and went down the hall into the buttery and found the meat, and ate his fill, and came away with the drink back to the Long-hoary man, who chuckled as he came and said: "Fill up now for thee and for me, and call a health to me and wish me somewhat" 🖋 "I wish thee luck," said Hallblithe, and drank. 🖋 Said the elder: "And I wish thee more wits; is luck all that thou mayst wish me? What luck may an outworn elder have?" 🖋 "Well then," quoth Hallblithe, "what shall I wish thee? Wouldst thou have me wish thee youth?" "Yea, certes," said the Long-hoary, "that and nought else." 🖋 "Youth then I wish thee, if it may avail thee aught," said Hallblithe, and he drank again therewith 🍂 "Nay, nay," said the old carle peevishly, "take a third cup, and wish me youth with no idle words tacked thereto" 🍃 Said Hallblithe raising the cup: "Herewith I wish thee youth!" and he drank 🍃 "Good is the wish," said the elder; "now ask thou the old carle whatso thou wilt."

AID Hallblithe: "What is this land called? "Son," said the other, "hast thou heard it called the Isle of Ransom?" "Yea," said Hallblithe, "but what wilt thou call it?" "By no other name," said the hoary carle. "It is far from other lands?" said Hallblithe. "Yea," said the carle, "when the light winds blow, & the ships sail slow." "What do ye who live here?" said Hallblithe. "How do ye live, what work win ye?" 🍂 "We win diverse work," said the elder, "but the gainfullest is robbing men by the high hand" 🍃 "Is it ye who have stolen from me the Hostage of the Rose?" said Hallblithe. Said the Long-hoary: "Maybe; I wot not; in diverse ways my kinsmen traffic, and they visit many lands. Why should they not have come to Cleveland also?" "Is she in this Isle, thou old runagate?" said Hallblithe 🍂 "She is not, thou young fool," said the elder 🍃 Then Hallblithe flushed red and spake: "Knowest thou the Puny Fox?" "How should I not?" said the carle, "since he is the son of one of my sons." "Dost thou call him a liar and a rogue?" said Hallblithe 🍂 The elder laughed; "Else were I a fool," said he; "there are few bigger liars or bigger rogues than the Puny Fox!" 🍃 "Is he here in this Isle?" said Hallblithe; "may I see him?" The old man laughed again, and said: "Nay, he is not here, unless he hath turned fool since yesterday: why should he abide thy sword, since he hath done what he would and brought thee hither?" 🍂 Then he laughed, as a hen cackles a long while, & then said: "What more wilt thou ask me?" But Hallblithe was very wroth: "It availeth nought to ask," he said; "& now I am in two minds whether I shall slay thee or not" 🍃 "That were a meet deed for a Raven, but not for a man," said the carle, "and thou that hast wished me luck! Ask, ask!" 🍂 But Hallblithe was silent a long while. Then the

carle said, "Another cup for the longer after youth!" Hallblithe filled, and gave to him, and the old man drank & said:
"Thou deemest us all liars in the Isle of Ransom because of
thy beguiling by the Puny Fox: but therein thou errest. The
Puny Fox is our chiefest liar, and doth for us the more part
of such work as we need: therefore, why should we others
lie. Ask, ask!" ✒ "Well then," said Hallblithe, "why did the
Puny Fox bewray me, and at whose bidding?" Said the elder:
"I know, but I will not tell thee. Is this a lie?" "Nay, I deem it
not," said Hallblithe: "But, tell me, is it verily true that my
troth-plight is not here, that I may ransom her?" ✒ Said the
Long-hoary: "I swear it by the Treasure of the Sea, that she
is not here: the tale was but a lie of the Puny Fox."

CHAPTER VII: A FEAST IN THE ISLE OF RANSOM

HALLBLITHE pondered his answer awhile with downcast eyes, & said at last: "Have ye a mind to ransom me, now that I have walked into the trap?" "There is no need to talk of ransom," said the elder; "thou mayst go out of this house when thou wilt, nor will any meddle with thee if thou strayest about the Isle, when I have set a mark on thee & given thee a token: nor wilt thou be hindered if thou hast a mind to leave the Isle, if thou canst find means thereto; moreover as long as thou art in the Isle, in this

house mayst thou abide, eating and drinking and resting
with us" 🌿 "How may I leave this," said Hallblithe 🌿
The elder laughed: "In a ship," said he. "And when," said
Hallblithe, "shall I find a ship that shall carry me?" Said
the old carle, "Whither wouldest thou, my son?" Hallblithe
was silent a while, thinking what answer he should make;
then he said: "I would go to the land of the Glittering
Plain." "Son, a ship shall not be lacking thee for that voyage," said the elder. "Thou mayst go to-morrow morn 🌿
And I bid thee abide here to-night, and thy cheer shall not
be ill. Yet if thou wilt believe my word, it will be well for
thee to say as little as thou mayst to any man here, & that
little as little proud as maybe: for our folk are short of
temper and thou knowest there is no might against many.
Indeed it is not unlike that they will not speak one word
to thee, and if that be so, thou hast no need to open thy
mouth to them. And now I will tell thee that it is good that
thou hast chosen to go to the Glittering Plain. For if thou
wert otherwise minded, I wot not how thou wouldest get
thee a keel to carry thee, & the wings have not yet begun
to sprout on thy shoulders, raven tho' thou be. Now I am
glad that thou art going thy ways to the Glittering Plain
to-morrow; for thou wilt be good company to me on the
way: and I deem that thou wilt be no churl when thou art
glad."

WHAT," said Hallblithe, "art thou wending thither, thou
old man?" 🌿 "Yea," said he, "nor shall any other be on
the ship save thou and I, & the mariners that waft us; &
they forsooth shall not go aland there. Why should not I go,
since there are men to bear me aboard?" 🌿 Said Hallblithe:
"And when thou art come aland there, what wilt thou do?"
🌿 "Thou shalt see, my son," said the Long-hoary. "It may be
that thy good wishes shall be of avail to me. But now since
all this may only be if I live through this night, & since my
heart hath been warmed by the good mead, and thy fellowship, and whereas I am somewhat sleepy, and it is long past
noon, go forth into the hall, & leave me to sleep, that I may

be as sound as eld will have me be to-morrow. And as for thee, folk, both men and women, shall presently come into the hall, & I deem not that any shall meddle with thee; but if so be that any challenge thee, whatsoever may be his words, answer thou to him, 'THE HOUSE OF THE UNDY-ING,' and there will be an end of it. Only look thou to it that no naked steel come out of thy scabbard 🖉 Go now, and if thou wilt, go out of doors; yet art thou safer within doors and nigher unto me."

SO Hallblithe went back into the main hall, & the sun had gotten round now, & was shining into the hall, through the clerestory windows, so that he saw clearly all that was therein. And he deemed the hall fairer within than without; & especially over the shut-beds were many stories carven in the panelling, and Hallblithe beheld them gladly. But of one thing he marvelled, that whereas he was in an island of the strong-thieves of the waters, and in their very home and chiefest habitation, there were no ships or seas pictured in that imagery, but fair groves and gardens, with flowery grass and fruited trees all about. And there were fair women abiding therein, and lovely young men, and warriors, and strange beasts and many marvels, and the ending of wrath and beginning of pleasure and the crowning of love. And amidst these was pictured oft and again a mighty king with a sword by his side and a crown on his head; and ever was he smiling & joyous, so that Hallblithe, when he looked on him, felt of better heart & smiled back on the carven image.

SO while Hallblithe looked on these things, & pondered his case carefully, all alone as he was in that alien hall, he heard a noise without of talking and laughter, and presently the pattering of feet therewith, and then women came into the hall, a score or more, some young, some old, some fair enough, and some hard-featured and uncomely, but all above the stature of the women whom he had seen in his own land 🖉 So he stood amidst the hall-floor and

abided them; and they saw him and his shining war-gear,
& ceased their talking and laughter, and drew round about
him, & gazed at him; but none said aught till an old crone
came forth from the ring, and said "Who art thou, standing
under weapons in our hall?" He knew not what to answer,
and held his peace; and she spake again: "Whither wouldest thou, what seekest thou?" 🖋 Then answered Hallblithe:
"THE HOUSE OF THE UNDYING." None answered, and
the other women all fell away from him at once, and went
about their business hither and thither through the hall.
But the old crone took him by the hand, & led him up to the
dais, and set him next to the midmost high-seat. Then she
made as if she would do off his war-gear, & he would not
gainsay her, though he deemed that foes might be anear;
for in sooth he trusted in the old carle that he would not
bewray him, and moreover he deemed it would be unmanly
not to take the risks of the guesting, according to the custom of that country 🖋 So she took his armour and his
weapons and bore them off to a shut-bed next to that
wherein lay the ancient man, and she laid the gear within
it, all save the spear, which she laid on the wall-pins above;
and she made signs to him that therein he was to lie; but
she spake no word to him. Then she brought him the hand-
washing water in a basin of latten, & a goodly towel
therewith, and when he had washed she went away from
him, but not far.

THIS while the other women were busy about the hall;
some swept the floor down, & when it was swept
strawed thereon rushes & wild thyme: some went into the
buttery and bore forth the boards and the trestles: some
went to the chests and brought out the rich hangings, the
goodly bankers and dorsars, & did them on the walls: some
bore in the stoups and horns and beakers, & some went their
ways and came not back a while, for they were busied about
the cooking. But whatever they did, none hailed him, or
heeded him more than if he had been an image, as he sat
there looking on. None save the old woman who brought him

the fore-supper, to wit a great horn of mead, and cakes and dried fish.

SO was the hall arrayed for the feast very fairly, & Hallblithe sat there while the sun westered and the house grew dim, and dark at last, and they lighted the candles up & down the hall. But a little after these were lit, a great horn was winded close without, and thereafter came the clatter of arms about the door, and exceeding tall weaponed men came in, one score and five, & strode two by two up to the foot of the dais, and stood there in a row. And Hallblithe deemed their war-gear exceeding good; they were all clad in ring-locked byrnies, and had steel helms on their heads with garlands of gold wrought about them and they bore spears in their hands, and white shields hung at their backs. Now came the women to them and unarmed them; and under their armour their raiment was black; but they had gold rings on their arms, and golden collars about their necks. So they strode up to the dais and took their places on the high-seat, not heeding Hallblithe any more than if he were an image of wood. Nevertheless that man sat next to him who was the chieftain of all and sat in the midmost high-seat; and he bore his sheathed sword in his hand and laid it on the board before him, and he was the only man of those chieftains who kept a weapon. But when these were set down, there was again a noise without, and there came in a throng of men armed and unarmed who took their places on the endlong benches up & down the hall; with these came women also, who most of them sat amongst the men, but some busied them with the serving: all these men were great of stature, but none so big as the chieftains on the high-seat.

NOW came the women in from the kitchen bearing the meat, whereof no little was flesh-meat, and all was of the best Hallblithe was duly served like the others, but still none spake to him or even looked on him; though amongst themselves they spoke in big, rough voices so that the rafters of the hall rang again 🍃 When they had eaten their fill the women filled round the cups and the horns to them, and those vessels were both great and goodly 🍃 But ere they fell to drinking uprose the chieftain who sat furthest from the midmost high-seat on the right & cried a health: "THE TREASURE OF THE SEA!" Then they all stood up and shouted, women as well as men, and emptied their horns and cups to that health. Then stood up the man furthest on the left and cried out, "Drink a health to the Undying King!" And again all men rose up and shouted ere they drank. Other healths they drank, as the "Cold Keel," the "Windworn Sail," the "Quivering Ash" and the "Furrowed Beach." And the wine and mead flowed like rivers in that hall of the Wild Men. As for Hallblithe, he drank what he would but stood not up, nor raised his cup to his lips when a health was drunk; for he knew not whether these men were his friends or his foes, and he deemed it would be little-minded to drink to their healths, lest he might be drinking death and confusion to his own kindred.

BUT when men had drunk awhile, again a horn blew at the nether end of the hall, & straightway folk arose from the endlong tables, and took away the boards and trestles, and cleared the floor and stood against the wall; then the big chieftain beside Hallblithe arose & cried out: "Now let man dance with maid, and be we merry! Music, strike up!" Then flew the fiddle-bows and twanged the harps, and the carles and queens stood forth on the floor; and all the women were clad in black raiment, albeit embroidered with knots and wreaths of flowers. A while they danced, & then suddenly the music fell, and they all went back to their places. Then the chieftain in the highseat arose and took a horn from his side, and blew a great blast on it that filled the hall; then he cried in a loud voice: "Be we merry! Let the champions come forth!"

EN shouted gleefully thereat, and straightway ran into the hall from out the screens three tall men clad all in black armour with naked swords in their hands, & stood amidst the hall-floor, somewhat on one side, & clashed their swords on their shields and cried out: "Come forth ye Champions of the Raven!" *Then* leapt Hallblithe from his seat and set his hand to his left side, but no sword was there; so he sat down again, remembering the warning of the Elder, and none heeded him *Then* there came into the hall slowly and mournfully three men-at-arms, clad and weaponed like the warriors of his folk, with the image of the Raven on their helms and shields. So Hallblithe refrained him, for besides that this seemed like to be a fair battle of three against three, he doubted some snare, and he determined to look on and abide *So* the champions fell to laying on strokes that were no child's play, though Hallblithe doubted if the edges bit, and it was but a little while before the Champions of the Raven fell one after another before the Wild Men, and folk drew them by the heels out into the buttery. Then arose great laughter and jeering, & exceeding wroth was Hallblithe; howbeit he refrained him because he remembered all he had to do. But the three Champions of the Sea strode round the hall, tossing up their swords & catching them as they fell, while the horns blew up behind them.

FTER a while the hall grew hushed, & the chieftain arose and cried: "Bring in now some sheaves of the harvest we win, we lads of the oar and the arrow!" *Then* was there a stir at the screen doors, and folk pressed forward to see, and, lo, there came forward a string of women, led in by two weaponed carles; and the women were a score in number, and they were barefoot and their hair hung loose and their gowns were ungirt, & they were chained together wrist to wrist; yet had they gold at arm and neck: there was silence in the hall when they stood amidst

of the floor 🍃 Then indeed Hallblithe could not refrain
himself, & he leapt from his seat & on to the board, and over
it, and ran down the hall, and came to those women and
looked them in the face one by one, while no man spake in the
hall. But the Hostage was not amongst them; nay forsooth,
they none of them favoured of the daughters of his people,
though they were comely and fair; so that again Hallblithe
doubted if this were aught but a feast-hall play done to anger
him; whereas there was but little grief in the faces of those
damsels, & more than one of them smiled wantonly in his face
as he looked on them 🍃 So he turned about and went back to
his seat, having said no word, & behind him arose much mocking and jeering; but it angered him little now; for he
remembered the rede of the elder & how that he had done
according to his bidding, so that he deemed the gain was his.
So sprang up talk in the hall betwixt man and man, folk drank
about and were merry, till the chieftain arose again and smote
the board with the flat of his sword, and cried out in a loud
and angry voice, so that all could hear: "Now let there be
music and minstrelsy ere we wend bedward!"

HEREWITH fell the hubbub of voices, and there
came forth three men with great harps, and a
fourth man with them, who was the minstrel; and
the harpers smote their harps so that the roof rang
therewith, and the noise, though it was great, was tuneable,
and when they had played thus a little while, they abated
their loudness somewhat, & the minstrel lifted his voice and
sang:

THE land lies black
With winter's lack,
The wind blows cold
Round field and fold;
All folk are within,
And but weaving they win.
Where from finger to finger

the shuttle flies fast,
And the eyes of the singer
look fain on the cast,
As he singeth the story
of summer undone
And the barley sheaves hoary
ripe under the sun.

THEN the maidens stay
The light-hung sley,
And the shuttles bide
By the blue web's side,
While hand in hand
With the carles they stand.
But ere to the measure
the fiddles strike up,
And the elders yet treasure
the last of the cup,
There stand they a-hearkening
the blast from the lift,
And e'en night is a-darkening
more under the drift.

THERE safe in the hall
They bless the wall,
And the roof o'er head,
Of the valiant stead;
And the hands they praise
Of the olden days.
Then through the storm's roaring
the fiddles break out,
And they think not of warring,
but cast away doubt,
And, man before maiden,
their feet tread the floor,
And their hearts are unladen
of all that they bore.

BUT what winds are o'er-cold
For the heart of the bold?
What seas are o'er-high
For the undoomed to die?
Dark night and dread wind,
But the haven we find.
Then ashore mid the flurry
of stone-washing surf!
Cloud-hounds the moon worry,
but light lies the turf;
Lo the long dale before us!
the lights at the end,
Though the night darkens o'er us,
bid whither to wend.

WHO beateth the door
By the foot-smitten floor?
What guests are these
From over the seas?
Take shield and sword
For their greeting-word.
Lo, lo, the dance ended!
lo, midst of the hall
The fallow blades blended!
lo, blood on the wall!
Who liveth, who dieth?
O men of the sea,
For peace the folk crieth;
our masters are ye.

NOW the dale lies grey
At the dawn of day;
And fair feet pass
O'er the wind-worn grass;
And they turn back to gaze
On the roof of old days.
Come tread ye the oaken-
floored hall of the sea!

Be your hearts yet unbroken;
so fair as ye be,
That kings are abiding
unwedded to gain
The news of our riding
the steeds of the main.

Much shouting and laughter arose at the song's end; and
men sprang up and waved their swords above the cups, while
Hallblithe sat scowling down on their merriment. Lastly
arose the chieftain and called out loudly for the good-night
cup, and it went round & all men drank. Then the horn blew
for bed, and the chieftains went to their chambers, and the
others went to the out-bowers or laid them down on the hall-
floor, and in a little while none stood upright thereon. So
Hallblithe arose, and went to the shut-bed appointed for him,
and laid him down and slept dreamlessly till the morning.

CHAPTER VIII: HALLBLITHE TAKETH SHIP AGAIN AWAY FROM THE ISLE OF RANSOM

HEN he awoke, the sun shone into the hall by the windows above the buttery, and there were but few folk left therein. But so soon as Hallblithe was clad, the old woman came to him, & took him by the hand, and led him to the board, and signed to him to eat of what was thereon; and he did so;

and by then he was done, came folk who went into the shut-bed where lay the Long-hoary, & they brought him forth bed and all and bare him out a-doors. Then the crone brought Hallblithe his arms, & he did on byrny and helm, girt his sword to his side, took his spear in his hand and went out a-doors; and there close by the porch lay the Long-hoary upon a horse-litter. So Hallblithe came up to him and gave him the sele of the day: & the elder said: "Good morrow, son, I am glad to see thee. Did they try thee hard last night?" And Hallblithe saw two of the carles that had borne out the elder, that they were talking together, and they looked on him and laughed mockingly; so he said to the elder: "Even fools may try a wise man, and so it befel last night. Yet, as thou seest, mumming hath not slain me" Said the old man: "What thou sawest was not all mumming; it was done according to our customs; and well nigh all of it had been done, even hadst thou not been there. Nay, I will tell thee; at some of our feasts it is not lawful to eat either for the chieftains or the carles, till a champion hath given forth a challenge, and been answered and met, & the battle fought to an end. But ye men, what hindereth you to go to the horses' heads & speed on the road the chieftain who is no longer way-worthy?"

SO they ran to the horses and set down the dale by the river-side, and just as Hallblithe was going to follow afoot, there came a swain from behind the house leading a red horse which he brought to Hallblithe as one who bids mount. So Hallblithe leapt into the saddle & at once caught up with the litter of the Long-hoary down along the river. They passed by no other house, save here & there a cot beside some fold or byre; they went easily, for the way was smooth by the river-side; so in less than two hours they came where the said river ran into the sea. There was no beach there, for the water was ten fathom deep close up to the lip of the land; but there was a great haven land-locked all but a narrow out-gate betwixt the sheer black cliffs. Many a great ship might have lain in that haven; but as now there was but one lying there, a round-ship not very great, but exceeding trim and meet for the sea.

THERE without more ado the carles took the elder from the litter and bore him aboard, and Hall-blithe followed him as if he had been so appointed. They laid the old man adown on the poop under a tilt of precious web, and so went aback by the way that they had come; and Hallblithe went & sat down beside the Long-hoary, who spake to him and said: "Seest thou, son, how easy it is for us twain to be shipped for the land whither we would go? But as easy as it is for thee to go thither whereas we are going, just so hard had it been for thee to go elsewhere. Moreover I must tell thee that though many an one of the Isle of Ransom desireth to go this voyage, there shall none else go, till the world is a year older, and he who shall go then shall be likest to me in all ways, both in eld and in fee-bleness, and in gibing speech, and all else; and now that I am gone, his name shall be the same as that whereby ye may call me to-day, and that is Grandfather. Art thou glad or sorry, Hallblithe?" *"Grandfather," said Hallblithe, "I can scarce tell thee: I move as one who hath no will to wend one way or other. Meseems I am drawn to go thither whereas we are going; therefore I deem that I shall find my beloved on the Glittering Plain: and whatever befalleth afterward, let it be as it will!" *"Tell me, my son," said the Grandfa-ther, "how many women are there in the world?" *"How may I tell thee?" said Hallblithe *"Well, then," said the elder, "how many exceeding fair women are there?" Said Hallblithe, "Indeed I wot not" *"How many of such hast thou seen?" said the Grandfather. "Many," said Hallblithe; "the daughters of my folk are fair, and there will be many other such amongst the aliens" * Then laughed the elder, and said: "Yet, my son, he who had been thy fellow since thy sundering from thy beloved, would have said that in thy deeming there is but one woman in the world; or at least one fair woman: is it not so?" * Then Hallblithe reddened at first, as though he were angry; then he said: "Yea, it is so."

Said the Grandfather in a musing way: "I wonder if before long I shall think of it as thou dost" 🍃 Then Hallblithe gazed at him marvelling, and studied to see wherein lay the gibe against himself; and the Grandfather beheld him, and laughed as well as he might, and said: "Son, son; didst thou not wish me youth?" "Yea," said Hallblithe, "but what ails thee to laugh so? What is it I have said or done?" "Nought, nought," said the elder, laughing still more, "only thou lookest so mazed. And who knoweth what thy wish may bring forth?"

WHEREAT was Hallblithe sore puzzled; but while he set himself to consider what the old carle might mean, uprose the hale and how of the mariners; they cast off the hawsers from the shore, ran out the sweeps, & drove the ship through the haven-gates. It was a bright sunny day; within, the green water was oily-smooth, without the rippling waves danced merrily under a light breeze, & Hallblithe deemed the wind to be fair; for the mariners shouted joyously and made all sail on the ship; and she lay over and sped through the waves, casting off the seas from her black bows. Soon were they clear of those swart cliffs, & it was but a little afterwards that the Isle of Ransom was grown deep blue behind them and far away.

CHAPTER IX: THEY COME TO THE LAND OF THE GLITTERING PLAIN

AS in the hall, so in the ship, Hallblithe noted that the folk were merry and of many words one with another, while to him no man cast a word save the Grandfather. As to Hallblithe, though he wondered much what all this betokened, & what the land was whereto he was wending, he was no man to fear an unboded peril; and he said to himself that whatever else betid, he should meet the Hostage on the Glittering Plain; so his heart rose and he was of good cheer, & as the Grandfather had foretold, he was a merry faring-fellow to him. Many a gibe the old man cast at him, and whiles Hallblithe gave him back as good as he took, and whiles he laughed as the stroke went home and silenced him; and whiles he understood nought of what the elder said. So wore the day and still the wind held fair, though it was light; and the sun set in a sky nigh cloudless, and there was nowhere any forecast of peril. But when night was come, Hallblithe lay down on a fair bed, which was dight for him in the poop, and he soon fell asleep and dreamed not save such dreams as are but made up of bygone memories, and betoken nought, & are not remembered.

WHEN he awoke, day lay broad on the sea, and the waves were little, the sky had but few clouds, the sun shone bright, and the air was warm and sweet-breathed 🍃 He looked aside and saw the old man sitting up in his bed as ghastly as a dead man dug up again: his bushy eye-brows were wrinkled over his bleared old eyes, the long white hair dangled forlorn from his gaunt head: yet was his face smiling and he looked as happy as the soul within him could make the half-dead body. He turned now to Hallblithe and said: "Thou art late awake: hadst thou been waking earlier, the sooner had thine heart been gladdened. Go forward now, and gaze thy fill and come and tell me thereof" 🍃 "Thou art happy, Grandfather," said Hallblithe, "what good tidings hath morn brought us?" 🍃 "The Land! the Land!" said the Long-hoary; "there are no longer tears in this old body, else should I be weeping for joy." 🍃 Said Hallblithe: "Art thou going to meet some one who shall make thee glad before thou diest, old man?"

SOME one?" said the elder; "what one? Are they not all gone? burned, and drowned, and slain and died abed? Some one, young man? Yea, forsooth some one indeed! Yea, the great warrior of the Wasters of the Shore; the Sea-eagle who bore the sword and the torch and the terror of the Ravagers over the coal-blue sea. It is myself, MYSELF that I shall find on the Land of the Glittering Plain, O young lover!"

Hallblithe looked on him wondering as he raised his wasted arms toward the bows of the ship pitching down the slope of the sunlit sea, or climbing up it. Then again the old man fell back on his bed & muttered: "What fool's work is this! that thou wilt draw me on to talk loud, and waste my body with lack of patience. I will talk with thee no more, lest my heart swell and break, & quench the little spark of life within me."

THEN Hallblithe arose to his feet, and stood looking at him, wondering so much at his words, that for a while he forgat the land which they were nearing, though he had caught glimpses of it, as the bows of the round-ship fell downward into the hollow of the sea. The wind was but light, as hath been said, and the waves little under it, but there was still a smooth swell of the sea which came of breezes now dead, & the ship wallowed thereon and sailed but slowly.

IN a while the old man opened his eyes again, and said in a low peevish voice: "Why standest thou staring at me? why hast thou not gone forward to look upon the land? True it is that ye Ravens are short of wits." Said Hallblithe: "Be not wrath, chieftain; I was wondering at thy words, which are exceeding marvellous; tell me more of this land of the Glittering Plain" Said the Grandfather: "Why should I tell it thee? ask of the mariners. They all know more than thou dost" "Thou knowest," said Hallblithe, "that these men speak not to me, and take no more heed of me than if I were an image which they were carrying to sell to the next mighty man they may hap on. Or tell me, thou old man," said he fiercely, "is it perchance a thrallmarket whereto they are bringing me? Have they sold her there, and will they sell me also in the same place, but into other hands?" "Tush!" said the Grandfather somewhat feebly, "this last word of thine is folly; there is no buying or selling in the land whereto we are bound. As to thine other word, that these men have no fellowship with thee, it is true: thou art my fellow and the fellow of none else aboard. Therefore if I feel might in me, maybe I will tell thee somewhat" 🖋 Then he raised his head a little and said: "The sun grows hot, the wind faileth us, & slow and slow are we sailing."

VEN as he spoke there was a stir amidships, and Hallblithe looked and beheld the mariners handling the sweeps, & settling themselves on the rowing-benches. Said the elder: "There is noise amidships, what are they doing?" 🖋 The old man raised himself a little again, and cried out in his shrill voice: "Good lads! brave lads! Thus would we do in the old time when we drew anear some shore, and the beacons were sending up smoke by day, and flame benights; & the shore-abiders did on their helms and trembled. Thrust her through, lads! Thrust her along!" 🖋 Then he fell back again, and said in a weak voice: "Make no more delay, guest, but go forward and look upon the land, and come back and tell me thereof, and then the tale may flow from me. Haste, haste!" 🖋 So Hallblithe went down from the poop, and in to the waist, where now the rowers were bending to their oars, and crying out fiercely as they tugged at the quivering ash; and he clomb on to the forecastle and went forward right to the dragon-head, and gazed long upon the land, while the dashing of the oar-blades made the semblance of a gale about the ship's black sides. Then he came back again to the Sea-eagle, who said to him: "Son, what hast thou seen?" 🖋 "Right ahead lieth the land, & it is still a good way off. High rise the mountains there, but by seeming there is no snow on them; and though they be blue they are not blue like the mountains of the Isle of Ransom. Also it seemed to me as if fair slopes of woodland and meadow come down to the edge of the sea. But it is yet far away" 🖋 "Yea," said the elder, "is it so? Then will I not wear myself with making words for thee. I will rest rather, and gather might. Come again when an hour hath worn, and tell me what thou seest; and may happen then thou shalt have my tale!" And he laid him down therewith and seemed to be asleep at once. And Hallblithe might not amend it; so he waited patiently till the hour had worn, and then went forward again, & looked long and carefully, & came back and said to the Sea-eagle, "The hour is worn."

HE old chieftain turned himself about and said "What hast thou seen?" *❧* Said Hallblithe: "The mountains are pale and high, and below them are hills dark with wood, and betwixt them and the sea is a fair space of meadowland, and methought it was wide" *❧* Said the old man: "Sawest thou a rocky skerry rising high out of the sea anigh the shore?" *❧* "Nay," said Hallblithe, "if there be, it is all blended with the meadows and the hills." Said the Sea-eagle: "Abide the wearing of another hour, & come and tell me again, and then I may have a gainful word for thee." And he fell asleep again *❧* But Hallblithe abided, and when the hour was worn, he went forward and stood on the forecastle. And this was the third shift of the rowers, and the stoutest men in the ship now held the oars in their hands, and the ship shook thro' all her length and breadth as they drave her over the waters.

O Hallblithe came aft to the old man and found him asleep; so he took him by the shoulder, and shook him and said: "Awake, faring-fellow, for the land is a-nigh" *❧* So the old man sat up and said: "What hast thou seen?" *❧* Said Hallblithe: "I have seen the peaks and cliffs of the far-off mountains; and below them are hills green with grass and dark with woods, and thence stretch soft green meadows down to the sea-strand, which is fair and smooth, and yellow" *❧* "Sawest thou the skerry?" said the Sea-eagle. "Yea, I saw it," said Hallblithe, "and it rises sheer from out the sea about a mile from the yellow strand; but its rocks are black, like the rocks of the Isle of Ransom" *❧* "Son," said the elder, "give me thine hands & raise me up a little." So Hallblithe took him and raised him up, so that he sat leaning against the pillows. And he looked not on Hallblithe, but on the bows of the ship, which now pitched but a little up and down, for the sea was laid quiet now. Then he cried in his shrill, piping voice: "It is the Land! It is the Land!"

BUT after a little while he turned to Hallblithe & spake: "Short is the tale to tell: thou hast wished me youth, and thy wish hath thriven; for to-day, ere the sun goes down, thou shalt see me as I was in the days when I reaped the harvest of the sea with sharp sword and hardy heart. For this is the land of the Undying King, who is our lord and our gift-giver; and to some he giveth the gift of youth renewed, and life that shall abide here the Gloom of the Gods. But none of us all may come to the Glittering Plain and the King Undying without turning the back for the last time on the Isle of Ransom: nor may any men of the Isle come hither save those who are of the House of the Sea-eagle, and few of those, save the chieftains of the House such as are they who sat by thee on the high-seat that even. Of these once in a while is chosen one of us, who is old and spent and past battle, and is borne to this land and the gift of the Undying. Forsooth some of us have no will to take the gift, for they say they are liefer to go to where they shall meet more of our kindred than dwell on the Glittering Plain and the Acre of the Undying; but as for me I was ever an overbearing and masterful man, and meseemeth it is well that I meet as few of our kindred as may be: for they are a strifeful race" *⃰* Hereat Hallblithe marvelled exceedingly, and he said: "And what am I in all this story? Why am I come hither with thy furtherance?" Said the Sea-eagle: "We had a charge from the Undying King concerning thee, that we should bring thee hither alive and well, if so be thou camest to the Isle of Ransom. For what cause we had the charge, I know not, nor do I greatly heed" *⃰* Said Hallblithe: "And shall I also have that gift of undying youth, and life while the world of men and gods endureth?" *⃰* "I must needs deem so," said the Sea-eagle, "so long as thou abidest on the Glittering Plain; and I see not how thou mayst ever escape thence" *⃰* Now Hallblithe heard him, how he said "escape," and thereat he was somewhat ill at ease, and stood and pondered a little.

At last he said: "Is this then all that thou hast to tell me concerning the Glittering Plain?" 🍃 "By the Treasure of the Sea!" said the elder, "I know no more of it. The living shall learn. But I suppose that thou mayst seek thy troth-plight maiden there all thou wilt. Or thou mayst pray the Undying King to have her thither to thee. What know I? At least, it is like that there shall be no lack of fair women there: or else the promise of youth renewed is nought and vain. Shall this not be enough for thee?" 🍃 "Nay," said Hallblithe. "What," said the elder, "must it be one woman only?" "One only," said Hallblithe 🍃 The old man laughed his thin mocking laugh, and said: "I will not assure thee but that the land of the Glittering Plain shall change all that for thee so soon as it touches the soles of thy feet" 🍃 Hallblithe looked at him steadily and smiled, and said: "Well is it then that I shall find the Hostage there; for then shall we be of one mind, either to sunder or to cleave together. It is well with me this day" 🍃 "And with me it shall be well ere long," said the Sea-eagle.

UT now the rowers ceased rowing and lay on their oars, and the shipmen cast anchor; for they were but a bow-shot from the shore, and the ship swung with the tide and lay side-long to the shore 🍃 Then said the Sea-eagle: "Look forth, shipmate, and tell me of the land" 🍃 And Hallblithe looked and said: "The yellow beach is sandy and shell-strewn, as I deem, and there is no great space of it betwixt the sea and the flowery grass; and a bowshot from the strand I see a little wood amidst which are fair trees blossoming" 🍃 "Seest thou any folk on the shore?" said the old man 🍃 "Yea," said Hallblithe, "close to the edge of the sea go four; & by seeming three are women, for their long gowns flutter in the wind. And one of these is clad in saffron colour, and another in white, and another in watchet; but the carle is clad in dark red; and their raiment is all glistening as with gold & gems; and by seeming they are looking at our ship as though they expected somewhat" 🍃 Said the Sea-eagle: "Why now do the shipmen tarry & have not made ready the skiff? Swillers and belly-gods they be; slothful swine that forget their chieftain."

BUT even as he spake came four of the shipmen, & without more ado took him up, bed and all, and bore him down into the waist of the ship, whereunder lay the skiff with four strong rowers lying on their oars. These men made no sign to Hallblithe, nor took any heed of him; but he caught up his spear, and followed them and stood by as they lowered the old man into the boat. Then he set his foot on the gunwale of the ship and leapt down lightly into the boat, and none hindered or helped him; and he stood upright in the boat, a goodly image of battle with the sun flashing back from his bright helm, his spear in his hand, his white shield at his back, and thereon the image of the Raven; but if he had been but a salt-boiling carle of the sea-side none would have heeded him less.

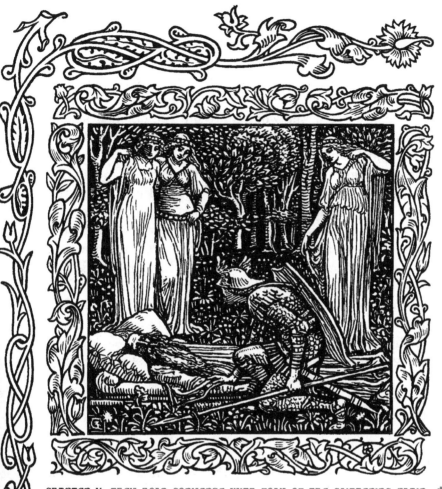

CHAPTER X: THEY HOLD CONVERSE WITH FOLK OF THE GLITTERING PLAIN

OW the rowers lifted the ash-blades, & fell to rowing towards shore: & almost with the first of their strokes, the Sea-eagle moaned out: "Would we were there, oh, would we were there! Cold groweth eld about my heart. Raven's Son, thou art standing up; tell me if thou canst see what these folk of the land are doing, and if any others have come thither?"

AID Hallblithe: "There are none others come, but kine and horses are feeding down the meadows. As to what those four are doing, the women are putting off their shoon, and girding up their raiment, as if they would wade the water toward us; and the carle, who was barefoot before, wendeth straight towards the sea, and there he standeth, for very little are the waves become" 🌿 The old man answered nothing, and did but groan for lack of patience; but presently when the water was yet waist deep the rowers stayed the skiff, and two of them slipped over the gunwale into the sea, and between them all they took up the chieftain on his bed and got him forth from the boat and went toward the strand with him; and the landsfolk met them where the water was shallower, and took him from their hands & bore him forth on to the yellow sand, & laid him down out of reach of the creeping ripple of the tide. Hallblithe withal slipped lightly out of the boat and waded the water after them. But the shipmen rowed back again to their ship, & presently Hall-blithe heard the hale and how, as they got up their anchor.

UT when Hallblithe was come ashore, and was drawn near the folk of the land, the women looked at him askance, and they laughed and said: "Welcome to thee also, O young man!" And he beheld them, and saw that they were of the stature of the maidens of his own land; they were exceeding fair of skin and shapely of fashion, so that the nakedness of their limbs under their girded gowns, and all glistening with the sea, was most lovely and dainty to behold. But Hallblithe knelt by the Sea-eagle to note how he fared, and said: "How is it with thee, O chieftain?" 🌿 The old man answered not a word, & he seemed to be asleep, and Hall-blithe deemed that his cheeks were ruddier and his skin less wasted and wrinkled than aforetime. Then spake one of those women: "Fear not, young man; he is well and will soon be better." Her voice was as sweet as a spring bird in the morning; she was white-skinned and dark-haired, and full sweetly fashioned; and she laughed on Hallblithe, but not mockingly; and her fellows also laughed, as though it were strange for him to be there. Then they did on their shoon again, and with the carle laid their hands to the bed whereon the old man lay, and lifted him up, & bore him forth on to the grass, turning their faces toward the flowery wood aforesaid; and they went a little way and then laid him down again and rested; and so on little by little, till they had brought him to the edge of the wood, and still he seemed to be asleep 🖉 Then the damsel who had spoken before, she with the dark hair, said to Hallblithe, "Although we have gazed on thee as if with wonder, this is not because we did not look to meet thee, but because thou art so fair and goodly a man: so abide thou here till we come back to thee from out of the wood." Therewith she stroked his hand, and with her fellows lifted the old man once more, & they bore him out of sight into the thicket.

BUT Hallblithe went to and fro a dozen paces from the wood, and looked across the flowery meads and deemed he had never seen any so fair. And afar off toward the hills he saw a great roof arising, and thought he could see men also; and nigher to him were kine pasturing, and horses also, whereof some drew anear him and stretched out their necks and gazed at him; and they were goodly after their kind; and a fair stream of water came round the corner out of the wood and down the meadows to the sea; and Hallblithe went thereto and could see that there was but little ebb and flow of the tide on that shore; for the water of the stream was clear as glass, and the grass and flowers grew right down to its water; so he put off his helm and drank of the stream and washed his face and his hands therein, and then did on his helm again and turned back again toward the wood, feeling very strong and merry; and he looked out seaward and saw the Ship of the Isle of Ransom lessening fast; for a little land wind had arisen and they had spread their sails to it; and he lay down on the grass till the four folk of the country came out of the wood again, after they had been gone somewhat less than an hour, but the Sea-eagle was not with them: and Hallblithe rose up and turned to them, and the carle saluted

him and departed, going straight toward that far-away roof
he had seen; and the women were left with Hallblithe, and
they looked at him and he at them as he stood leaning on his
spear.

HEN said the black-haired damsel: "True it is, O Spearman, that if we did not know of thee, our wonder would
be great that a man so young & lucky-looking should have
sought hither" ✿ "I wot not why thou shouldest wonder,"
said Hallblithe; "I will tell thee presently wherefore I come
hither. But tell me, is this the Land of the Glittering Plain?"
✿ Even so," said the damsel, "dost thou not see how the sun
shineth on it? Just so it shineth in the season that other
folks call winter" ✿ "Some such marvel I thought to hear
of," said he; "for I have been told that the land is marvellous;
and fair though these meadows be, they are not marvellous
to look on now: they are like other lands, though it maybe,
fairer" ✿ "That may be," she said; "we have nought but
hearsay of other lands. If we ever knew them we have forgotten them" ✿ Said Hallblithe, "Is this land called also the
Acre of the Undying?"

S he spake the words the smile faded from the damsel's
face; she and her fellows grew pale, and she said: "Hold
thy peace of such words! They are not lawful for any man to
utter here. Yet mayst thou call it the Land of the Living." ✿
He said: "I crave pardon for the rash word" ✿ Then they
smiled again, and drew near to him, and caressed him with
their hands, and looked on him lovingly; but he drew a little
aback from them and said: "I have come hither seeking something which I have lost, the lack whereof grieveth me" ✿
Quoth the damsel, drawing nearer to him again, "Mayst thou
find it, thou lovely man, and whatsoever else thou desirest."

HEN he said: "Hath a woman named the Hostage been
brought hither of late days? A fair woman, bright-haired
and grey-eyed, kind of countenance, soft of speech, yet out-
spoken and nought timorous; tall according to our stature,

but very goodly of fashion; a woman of the House of the Rose, and my trothplight maiden" 🖉 They looked on each other and shook their heads, and the black-haired damsel spake: "We know of no such a woman, nor of the kindred which thou namest" 🖉 Then his countenance fell, and became piteous with desire and grief, and he bent his brows upon them, for they seemed to him light-minded & careless, though they were lovely.

UT they shrank from him trembling, and drew aback; for they had all been standing close to him, beholding him with love, and she who had spoken most had been holding his left hand fondly. But now she said: "Nay, look not on us so bitterly! If the woman be not in the land, this cometh not of our malice. Yet maybe she is here. For such as come hither keep not their old names, and soon forget them what they were. Thou shalt go with us to the King, and he shall do for thee what thou wilt; for he is exceeding mighty" 🖉 Then was Hallblithe appeased somewhat; and he said: "Are there many women in the land?" 🖉 "Yea, many," said that damsel 🖉 "And many that are as fair as ye be?" said he. Then they laughed and were glad, and drew near to him again and took his hands & kissed them; and the black-haired damsel said: "Yea, yea, there be many as fair as we be, and some fairer," and she laughed 🖉 "And that King of yours," said he, "how do ye name him?" "He is the King," said the damsel. "Hath he no other name?" said Hallblithe. "We may not utter it," she said; "but thou shalt see him soon, that there is nought but good in him and mightiness."

CHAPTER XI: THE SEA-EAGLE RENEWETH HIS LIFE

UT while they spake together thus, came a man from out of the wood very tall of stature, red-bearded and black-haired, ruddy-cheeked, full-limbed, most joyous of aspect; a man by seeming of five and thirty winters. He strode straight up to Hallblithe, and cast his arms about him, and kissed his cheek, as if he had been an old and dear friend newly come from over seas Hallblithe wondered and laughed, and said: "Who art thou that deemest me so dear?" Said the man: "Short is thy memory, Son of the Raven, that thou in so little space hast forgotten thy shipmate and thy faring-fellow; who gave thee meat and drink and good rede in the Hall of the Ravagers." Therewith he laughed

& joyously turned about to the three maidens and took them by the hands and kissed their lips, while they fawned upon him lovingly 🖃 Then said Hallblithe: "Hast thou verily gotten thy youth again, which thou badest me wish thee?"

"YEA, in good sooth," said the red-bearded man; "I am the Sea-eagle of old days; and I have gotten my youth, and love therewithal, and somewhat to love moreover." Therewith he turned to the fairest of the damsels, and she was white-skinned and fragrant as the lily, rose-cheeked and slender, and the wind played with the long locks of her golden hair, which hung down below her knees; so he cast his arms about her and strained her to his bosom, and kissed her face many times, and she nothing loth, but caressing him with lips and hand. But the other two damsels stood by smiling and joyous: and they clapped their hands together and kissed each other for joy of the new lover; and at last fell to dancing and skipping about them like young lambs in the meadows of Spring-tide. But amongst them all, stood up Hallblithe leaning on his spear with smiling lips and knitted brow; for he was pondering in his mind in what wise he might further his quest 🖃 But after they had danced a while the Sea-eagle left his love that he had chosen & took a hand of either of the two damsels, & led them tripping up to Hallblithe, and cried out: "Choose thou, Raven's baby, which of these twain thou wilt have to thy mate; for scarcely shalt thou see better or fairer" 🖃 But Hallblithe looked on them proudly and sternly, and the black-haired damsel hung down her head before him and said softly: "Nay, nay, sea-warrior; this one is too lovely to be our mate. Sweeter love abides him, and lips more longed for."

THEN stirred Hallblithe's heart within him and he said: "O Eagle of the Sea, thou hast thy youth again: what then wilt thou do with it? Wilt thou not weary for the moonlit main, and the washing of waves and the dashing of spray, and thy fellows all glistering with the brine? Where now shall be the alien shores before thee, and the landing for fame, and departure for the gain of goods? Wilt thou forget the ship's black side, and the dripping of the windward oars, as the squall falleth on when the sun hath arisen, & the sail tuggeth hard on the sheet, and the ship lieth over and the lads shout against the whistle of the wind? Has the spear fallen from thine hand, & hast thou buried the sword of thy fathers in the grave from which thy body hath escaped? What art thou, O Warrior, in the land of the alien & the King? Who shall heed thee or tell the tale of thy glory, which thou hast covered over with the hand of a light woman, whom thy kindred knoweth not, and who was not born in a house wherefrom it hath been appointed thee from of old to take the pleasure of woman? Whose thrall art thou now, thou lifter of the spoil, thou scarer of the free-born? The bidding of what lord or King wilt thou do, O Chieftain, that thou mayst eat thy meat in the morning and lie soft in thy bed in the evening?" "O Warrior of the Ravagers, here stand I, Hallblithe of the Raven, and I am come into an alien land beset with marvels to seek mine own, and find that which is dearest to mine heart; to wit, my trothplight maiden, the Hostage of the Rose, the fair woman who shall lie in my bed, and bear me children, and stand by me in field and fold, by thwart and gunwale, before the bow and the spear, by the flickering of the cooking-fire, and amidst the blaze of the burning hall, and beside the bale-fire of the warrior of the Raven. O Sea-eagle, my guester amongst the foemen, my fellow-farer and shipmate, say now once for all whether thou wilt help me in my quest, or fall off from me as a dastard?"

AGAIN the maidens shrank before his clear and high-raised voice, & they trembled and grew pale 🌸 But the Sea-eagle laughed from a countenance kind with joy, and said: "Child of the Raven, thy words are good and manly: but it availeth nought in this land, & I wot not how thou wilt fare, or why thou hast been sent amongst us. What wilt thou do? Hadst thou spoken these words to the Long-hoary, the Grandfather, yesterday, his ears would have been deaf to them; and now that thou speakest them to the Sea-eagle, this joyous man on the Glittering Plain, he cannot do according to them, for there is no other land than this which can hold him. Here he is strong and stark, and full of joy and love; but otherwhere he would be but a gibbering ghost drifting down the wind of night. Therefore in whatsoever thou mayst do within this land I will stand by thee and help thee; but not one inch beyond it may my foot go, whether it be down into the brine of the sea, or up into the clefts of the mountains which are the wall of this goodly land. Thou hast been my shipmate and I love thee, I am thy friend; but here in this land must needs be the love and the friendship. For no ghost can love thee, no ghost may help thee. And as to what thou sayest concerning the days gone past and our joys upon the tumbling sea, true it is that those days were good and lovely; but they are dead and gone like the lads who sat on the thwart beside us, & the maidens who took our hands in the hall to lead us to the chamber. Other days have come in their stead, & other friends shall cherish us. What then? Shall we wound the living to pleasure the dead, who cannot heed it? Shall we curse the Yuletide, and cast foul water on the Holy Hearth of the winter feast, because the summer once was fair and the days flit & the times change? Now let us be glad! For life liveth.”

THEREWITH he turned about to his damsel and kissed her on the mouth. But Hallblithe’s face was grown sad and stern, and he spake slowly & heavily: “So is it, shipmate, that whereas thou sayest that the days flit, for thee they shall flit no more; & the day may come for thee when thou shalt be weary, & know it, and long for the lost which thou hast forgotten. But hereof it availeth nought for me to speak any longer, for thine ears are deaf to these words, and thou wilt not hear them. Therefore I say no more save that I thank thee for thy help whatsoever it may be; and I will take it, for the day’s work lieth before me, & I begin to think that it may be heavy enough.”

HE women yet looked downcast, and as if they would be gone out of earshot; but the Sea-eagle laughed as one who is well content, & said: "Thou thyself wilt make it hard for thyself after the wont of thy proud & haughty race; but for me nothing is hard any longer; neither thy scorn nor thy forebodings of evil. Be thou my friend as much as thou canst, and I will be thine wholly. Now ye women, whither will ye lead us? For I am ready to see any new thing ye will show us" ✒ Said his damsel: "We will take you to the King, that your hearts may be the more gladdened. And as for thy friend the Spearman, O Sea-warrior, let not his heart be downcast. Who wotteth but that these two desires, the desire of his heart, and the desire of a heart for him, may not be one and the same desire, so that he shall be fully satisfied?" As she spoke she looked sidelong at Hallblithe, with shy and wheedling eyes; and he wondered at her word, and a new hope sprang up in his heart that he was presently to be brought face to face with the Hostage, and that this was that love, sweeter than their love, which abode in him, and his heart became lighter, and his visage cleared.

CHAPTER XII: THEY LOOK ON THE KING OF THE GLITTERING PLAIN ✿✿

S O now the women led them along up the stream, and Hallblithe went side by side by the Sea-eagle; but the women had become altogether merry again, and played

& ran about them as gamesome as young goats; and they
waded the shallows of the clear bright stream bare-foot to
wash their limbs of the seabrine, and strayed about the
meadows, plucking the flowers and making them wreaths
and chaplets, which they did upon themselves & the Sea-
eagle; but Hallblithe they touched not, for still they feared
him. They went on as the stream led them up toward the
hills, and ever were the meads about them as fair and flowery as might be. Folk they saw afar off, but fell in with none
for a good while, saving a man and a maid clad lightly as for
mid-summer days, who were wandering together lovingly
and happily by the streamside, and who gazed wonderingly
on the stark Sea-eagle, and on Hallblithe with his glittering
spear. The black-haired damsel greeted these twain and
spake something to them, and they laughed merrily, and the
man stooped down amongst the grasses and blossoms of the
bank, and drew forth a basket, and spread dainty victuals on
the grass under a willow-tree, and bade them be his guests
that fair afternoon. So they sat down there above the glistering stream & ate and drank and were merry. Thereafter the
new-comers and their way-leaders departed with kind words,
and still set their faces towards the hills.

AT last they saw before them a little wooded hill,
and underneath it something red and shining, &
other coloured things gleaming in the sun about it.
Then said the Sea-eagle: "What have we yonder?"
Said his damsel: "That is the pavilion of the King; and about
it are the tents and tilts of our folk who are of his fellowship:
for oft he abideth in the fields with them, though he hath
houses and halls as fair as the heart of man can conceive."
"Hath he no foemen to fear?" said the Sea-eagle. "How should
that be?" said the damsel. "If perchance any came into this
land to bring war upon him, their battle-anger should depart
when once the bliss of the Glittering Plain had entered into
their souls, and they would ask for nought but leave to abide
here and be happy. Yet I trow that if he had foemen he could
crush them as easily as I set my foot on this daisy."

SO as they went on they fell in with many folk, men and women, sporting & playing in the fields; and there was no semblance of eld on any of them, and no scar or blemish or feebleness of body or sadness of countenance; nor did any bear a weapon or any piece of armour. Now some of them gathered about the new-corners, and wondered at Hallblithe and his long spear and shining helm and dark grey byrny; but none asked concerning them, for all knew that they were folk new come to the bliss of the Glittering Plain. So they passed amidst these fair folk little hindered by them, & into Hallblithe's thoughts it came how joyous the fellowship of such should be and how his heart should be raised by the sight of them, if only his troth-plight maiden were by his side.

THUS then they came to the King's pavilion, where it stood in a bight of the meadow-land at the foot of the hill, with the wood about it on three sides. So fair a house Hallblithe deemed he had never seen; for it was wrought all over with histories and flowers, and with hems sewn with gold and with orphreys of gold and pearl and gems 🖋 There in the door of it sat the King of the Land in an ivory chair; he was clad in golden gown, girt with a girdle of gems, & had his crown on his head and his sword by his side. For this was the hour wherein he heard what any of his folk would say to him, and for that very end he sat there in the door of his tent, and folk were standing before him, & sitting and lying on the grass round about; and now one, now another, came up to him and spoke before him 🖋 His face shone like a star; it was exceeding beauteous, and as kind as the even of May in the gardens of the happy, when the scent of the eglantine fills all the air. When he spoke his voice was so sweet that all hearts were ravished, and none might gainsay him.

BUT when Hallblithe set eyes on him, he knew at once that this was he whose carven image he had seen in the hall of the Ravagers, and his heart beat fast, and he said to himself: "Hold up thine head now, O Son of the Raven, strengthen thine heart, and let no man or god cow thee. For how can thine heart change, which bade thee go to the house wherefrom it was due to thee to take the pleasure of woman, and there to pledge thy faith & troth to her that loveth thee most, and hankereth for thee day by day and hour by hour, so that great is the love that we twain have builded up." Now they drew nigh, for folk fell back before them to the right and left, as before men who are new come and have much to do; so that there was nought between them and the face of the King. But he smiled upon them so that he cheered their hearts with the hope of fulfilment of their desires, and he said:

WELCOME, children! Who be these whom ye have brought hither for the increase of our joy? Who is this tall, ruddy-faced, joyous man so meet for the bliss of the Glittering Plain? And who is this goodly and lovely young man, who beareth weapons amidst our peace, and whose face is sad and stern beneath the gleaming of his helm?" 🍂 Said the dark-haired damsel: "O King! O Gift-giver and assurer of joy! this tall one is he who was once oppressed by eld, and who hath come hither to thee from the Isle of Ransom, according to the custom of the land." Said the King: "Tall man, it is well that thou art come. Now are thy days changed and thou yet alive. For thee battle is ended, and therewith the reward of battle, which the warrior remembereth not amidst the hard hand-play: peace hath begun, and thou needest not be careful for the endurance thereof: for in this land no man hath a lack which he may not satisfy without taking aught from any other. I deem not that thine heart may conceive a desire which I shall not fulfil for thee, or crave a gift which I shall not give thee" 🍂 Then the Sea-eagle laughed for joy, and turned his head this way and that, so that he might the better take to him the smiles of all those that stood around 🍂 Then the King said to Hallblithe: "Thou also art welcome; I know thee who thou art: meseemeth great joy awaiteth thee, and I will fulfil thy desire to the uttermost" 🍂 Said

Hallblithe: "O great King of a happy land, I ask of thee nought save that which none shall withhold from me uncursed" 🖊 "I will give it to thee," said the King, "and thou shalt bless me. But what is it which thou wouldst? What more canst thou have than the Gifts of the land?"

SAID Hallblithe: "I came hither seeking no gifts, but to have mine own again; and that is the bodily love of my troth-plight maiden. They stole her from me, & me from her; for she loved me. I went down to the sea-side and found her not, nor the ship which had borne her away. I sailed from thence to the Isle of Ransom, for they told me that there I should buy her for a price; neither was her body there. But her image came to me in a dream of the night, and bade me seek to her hither. Therefore, O King, if she be here in the land, show me how I shall find her, and if she be not here, show me how I may depart to seek her otherwhere. This is all my asking" 🖊 Said the King: "Thy desire shall be satisfied; thou shalt have the woman who would have thee, and whom thou shouldst have" 🖊 Hallblithe was gladdened beyond measure by that word; and now did the King seem to him a comfort & a solace to every heart, even as he had deemed of his carven image in the Hall of the Ravagers; and he thanked him, & blessed him 🖊 But the King bade him abide by him that night, and feast with him. "And on the morrow," said he, "thou shalt go thy ways to look on her whom thou oughtest to love."

THEREWITH was come the eventide & beginning of night, warm and fragrant and bright with the twinkling of stars, and they went into the King's pavilion, & there was the feast as fair and dainty as might be; and Hallblithe had meat from the King's own dish, and drink from his cup; but the meat had no savour to him & the drink no delight, because of the longing that possessed him. And when the feast was done, the damsels led Hallblithe to his bed in a fair tent strewn with gold about his head like the starry night, and he lay down and slept for sheer weariness of body.

CHAPTER XIII: HALLBLITHE BEHOLDETH THE WOMAN WHO LOVETH HIM ❀❀

BUT on the morrow the men arose, & the Sea-eagle and his damsel came to Hallblithe; for the other two damsels were departed, and the Sea-eagle said to him: "Here am I well

honoured and measurelessly happy; and I have a message
for thee from the King" 🖋 "What is it?" said Hallblithe; but
he deemed that he knew what it would be, and he reddened
for the joy of his assured hope 🖋 Said the Sea-eagle: "Joy to
thee, O shipmate! I am to take thee to the place where thy
beloved abideth, & there shalt thou see her, but not so as she
can see thee; & thereafter shalt thou go to the King, that
thou mayst tell him if she shall accomplish thy desire" 🖋
Then was Hallblithe glad beyond measure, & his heart
danced within him, & he deemed it but meet that the others
should be so joyous and blithe with him, for they led him
along without any delay, and were glad at his rejoicing; and
words failed him to tell of his gladness.

BUT as he went, the thoughts of his coming converse
with his beloved curled sweetly round his heart, so that
scarce anything had seemed so sweet to him before; & he fell
a-pondering what they twain, he and the Hostage, should do
when they came together again; whether they should abide
on the Glittering Plain, or go back again to Cleveland by the
Sea and dwell in the House of the Kindred; and for his part
he yearned to behold the roof of his fathers and to tread the
meadow which his scythe had swept, and the acres where his
hook had smitten the wheat. But he said to himself, "I will
wait till I hear her desire hereon" 🖋 Now they went into the
wood at the back of the King's pavilion and through it, and
so over the hill, and beyond it came into a land of hills and
dales exceeding fair and lovely; and a river wound about the
dales, lapping in turn the feet of one hill-side or the other; &
in each dale (for they passed through two) was a goodly
house of men, and tillage about it, and vineyards and
orchards. They went all day till the sun was near setting,
and were not weary, for they turned into the houses by the
way when they would, and had good welcome, & meat and
drink and what they would of the folk that dwelt there. Thus
anigh sunset they came into a dale fairer than either of the
others, & nigh to the end where they had entered it was an
exceeding goodly house. Then said the damsel: "We are

nigh-hand to our journey's end; let us sit down on the grass
by this river-side whilst I tell thee the tale which the King
would have thee know."

SO they sat down on the grass beside the brimming
river, scant two bowshots from that fair house, & the
damsel said, reading from a scroll which she drew from her
bosom: "O Spearman, in yonder house dwelleth the woman
foredoomed to love thee: if thou wouldst see her, go thitherward, following the path which turneth from the river-side
by yonder oak-tree, and thou shalt presently come to a
thicket of bay-trees at the edge of an apple-orchard, whose
trees are blossoming; abide thou hidden by the bay-leaves,
and thou shalt see maidens come into the orchard, and at
last one fairer than all the others. This shall be thy love
fore-doomed, and none other; and thou shalt know her by
this token, that when she hath set her down on the grass
beside the bay-tree, she shall say to her maidens: 'Bring me
now the book wherein is the image of my beloved, that I
may solace myself with beholding it before the sun goes
down and the night cometh.'"

NOW Hallblithe was troubled when she read out
these words, and he said: "What is this tale about
a book? I know not of any book that lieth betwixt
me & my beloved" ⚔ "O Spearman," said the
damsel, "I may tell thee no more, because I know no more.
But keep up thine heart! For dost thou know any more than
I do what hath befallen thy beloved since thou wert sundered from her? and why should not this matter of the book
be one of the things that hath befallen her? Go now with joy,
and come again blessing us" ⚔ "Yea, go, faring-fellow," said
the Sea-eagle, "and come back joyful, that we may all be
merry together. And we will abide thee here."

HALLBLITHE foreboded evil, but he held his peace and
went his ways down the path by the oak-tree; and they
abode there by the water-side, and were very merry talking

of this and that (but no whit of Hallblithe), and kissing and
caressing each other; so that it seemed but a little while to
them ere they saw Hallblithe coming back by the oak-tree.
He went slowly, hanging his head like a man sore-burdened
with grief: thus he came up to them, and stood there above
them as they lay on the fragrant grass, and he saying no
word and looking so sad and sorry, and withal so fell, that
they feared his grief and his anger, and would fain have been
away from him; so that they durst not ask him a question for
a long while, & the sun sank below the hill while they abided
thus.

HEN all trembling the damsel spake to the Sea-eagle:
"Speak to him, dear friend, else must I flee away, for I
fear his silence" 🖋 Quoth the Sea-eagle: "Shipmate and
friend, what hath betided? How art thou? May we hearken,
and mayhappen amend it?" 🖋 Then Hallblithe cast himself
adown on the grass & said: "I am accursed and beguiled; and
I wander round and round in a tangle that I may not escape
from. I am not far from deeming that this is a land of dreams
made for my beguiling. Or has the earth become so full of
lies, that there is no room amidst them for a true man to
stand upon his feet & go his ways?" 🖋 Said the Sea-eagle:
"Thou shalt tell us of what hath betid, and so ease the sorrow of thy soul if thou wilt. Or if thou wilt, thou shalt nurse
thy sorrow in thine heart and tell no man. Do what thou
wilt; am I not become thy friend?"

AID Hallblithe: "I will tell you twain the tidings, and
thereafter ask me no more concerning them. Hearken.
I went whereas ye bade me, and hid myself in the bay-tree
thicket; and there came maidens into the blossoming orchard
& made a resting-place with silken cushions close to where I
was lurking, & stood about as though they were looking for
some one to come 🖋 In a little time came two more maidens, and betwixt them one so much fairer than any there,
that my heart sank within me: whereas I deemed because of
her fairness that this would be the foredoomed love whereof

ye spake, and lo, she was in nought like to my troth-plight maiden, save that she was exceeding beauteous: nevertheless, heart-sick as I was, I determined to abide the token that ye told me of. So she lay down amidst those cushions, and I beheld her that she was sad of countenance; and she was so near to me that I could see the tears welling into her eyes, and running down her cheeks; so that I should have grieved sorely for her had I not been grieving so sorely for myself. For presently she sat up and said 'O maiden, bring me hither the book wherein is the image of my beloved, that I may behold it in this season of sunset wherein I first beheld it; that I may fill my heart with the sight thereof before the sun is gone and the dark night come' 🖋 "Then indeed my heart died within me when I wotted that this was the love whereof the King spake, that he would give to me, and she not mine own beloved, yet I could not choose but abide and look on a while, and she being one that any man might love beyond measure 🖋 Now a maiden went away into the house and came back again with a book covered with gold set with gems; and the fair woman took it and opened it, and I was so near to her that I saw every leaf clearly as she turned the leaves. And in that book were pictures of many things, as flaming mountains, and castles of war, and ships upon the sea, but chiefly of fair women, and queens, and warriors and kings; and it was done in gold & azure and cinnabar & minium 🖋 So she turned the leaves, till she came to one whereon was pictured none other than myself, and over against me was the image of mine own beloved, the Hostage of the Rose, as if she were alive, so that the heart within me swelled with the sobbing which I must needs refrain, which grieved me like a sword-stroke. Shame also took hold of me as the fair woman spoke to my painted image, and I lying well-nigh within touch of her hand; but she said: 'O my beloved, why dost thou delay to come to me? For I deemed that this eve at least thou wouldst come, so many & strong as are the meshes of love which we have cast about thy feet. Oh come to-morrow at the least and latest, or what shall I do, and wherewith shall I quench the grief of my heart? Or

else why am I the daughter of the Undying King, the Lord
of the Treasure of the Sea? Why have they wrought new
marvels for me, and compelled the Ravagers of the Coasts to
serve me, and sent false dreams flitting on the wings of the
night? Yea, why is the earth fair and fruitful, and the heavens kind above it, if thou comest not to-night, nor to-morrow,
nor the day after? And I the daughter of the Undying, on
whom the days shall grow and grow as the grains of sand
which the wind heaps up above the sea-beach. And life shall
grow huger and more hideous round about the lonely one,
like the ling-worm laid upon the gold, that waxeth thereby,
till it lies all round about the house of the queen entrapped,
the moveless unending ring of the years that change not'
"So she spake till the weeping ended her words, and I was all
abashed with shame and pale with anguish. I stole quietly
from my lair unheeded of any, save that one damsel said
that a rabbit ran in the hedge, and another that a blackbird
stirred in the thicket. Behold me, then, that my quest beginneth again amidst the tangle of lies whereinto I have been
entrapped."

CHAPTER XIV: HALLBLITHE HAS SPEECH WITH THE KING AGAIN

E stood up when he had made an end, as a man ready for the road; but they lay there downcast and abashed, and had no words to answer him *❧* For the Sea-eagle was sorry that his faring-fellow was hapless, & was sorry that he was sorry; and as for the damsel, she had not known but that she was leading the goodly Spearman to the fulfilment of his heart's desire. Albeit after a while she spake again and said: "Dear friends, day is gone and night is at hand; now to-night it were ill lodging at yonder house; & the next house on our backward road is over far for wayworn folk. But hard by through the thicket is a fair little

wood-lawn, by the lip of a pool in the stream wherein we
may bathe us to-morrow morning; and it is grassy and flowery and sheltered from all winds that blow, and I have victual
enough in my wallet. Let us sup and rest there under the
bare heaven, as oft is the wont of us in this land; and on the
morrow early we will arise and get us back again to Wood-
end, where yet the King abideth, & there shalt thou talk to
him again, O Spearman" 🖋 Said Hallblithe: "Take me
whither ye will; but now nought availeth. I am a captive in a
land of lies, & here most like shall I live betrayed and die
hapless." "Hold thy peace, dear friend, of such words as those
last," said she, "or I must needs flee from thee, for they hurt
me sorely. Come now to this pleasant place" 🖋 She took him
by the hand and looked kindly on him, and the Sea-eagle followed him, murmuring an old song of the harvest-field, and
they went together by a path through a thicket of whitethorn
till they came unto a grassy place. There then they sat them
down, and ate and drank what they would, sitting by the lip
of the pool till a waning moon was bright over their heads.
And Hallblithe made no semblance of content; but the
Sea-eagle and his damsel were grown merry again, and
talked and sang together like autumn stares, with the kissing and caressing of lovers 🖋 So at last those twain lay
down amongst the flowers, and slept in each other's arms;
but Hallblithe betook him to the brake a little aloof, and lay
down, but slept not till morning was at hand, when slumber
and confused dreams overtook him.

HE was awaked from his sleep by the damsel, who came
pushing through the thicket all fresh and rosy from the
river, and roused him, and said: "Awake now, Spearman,
that we may take our pleasure in the sun; for he is high in
the heavens now, and all the land laughs beneath him" 🖋
Her eyes glittered as she spoke, and her limbs moved under
her raiment as though she would presently fall to dancing
for very joy. But Hallblithe arose wearily, and gave her back
no smile in answer, but thrust through the thicket to the
water, and washed the night from off him, and so came back

to the twain as they sat dallying together over their breakfast. He would not sit down by them, but ate a morsel of bread as he stood, and said: "Tell me how I can soonest find the King: I bid you not lead me thither, but let me go my ways alone. For with me time presses, and with you meseemeth time is nought. Neither am I a meet fellow for the happy" 🌿 But the Sea-eagle sprang up, and swore with a great oath that he would nowise leave his shipmate in the lurch. And the damsel said: "Fair man, I had best go with thee; I shall not hinder thee, but further thee rather, so that thou shalt make one day's journey of two" 🌿 And she put forth her hand to him, and caressed him smiling, & fawned upon him, and he heeded it little, but hung not aback from them since they were ready for the road: so they set forth all three together.

THEY made such diligence on the backward road that the sun was not set by then they came to Wood-end; and there was the King sitting in the door of his pavilion. Thither went Hallblithe straight, and thrust through the throng, and stood before the King; who greeted him kindly, and was no less sweet of face than on that other day 🌿 Hallblithe hailed him not, but said: "King, look on my anguish, and if thou art other than a king of dreams and lies, play no longer with me, but tell me straight out if thou knowest of my troth-plight maiden, whether she is in this land or not" 🌿 Then the King smiled on him and said: "True it is that I know of her; yet know I not whether she is in this land or not" 🌿 "King," said Hallblithe, "wilt thou bring us together and stay my heart's bleeding?" 🌿 Said the King: "I cannot, since I know not where she is" 🌿 "Why didst thou lie to me the other day?" said Hallblithe 🌿 "I lied not," said the King; "I bade bring thee to the woman that loved thee, and whom thou shouldst love; and that is my daughter. And look thou! Even as I may not bring thee to thine earthly love, so couldst thou not make thyself manifest before my daughter, and become her deathless love. Is it not enough?" 🌿 He spake sternly for all that he smiled, and Hallblithe said: "O

King, have pity on me!" 🖋 "Yea," said the King; "pity thee I do: but I will live despite thy sorrow; my pity of thee shall not slay me, or make thee happy. Even in such wise didst thou pity my daughter" 🖋 Said Hallblithe: "Thou art mighty, O King, and maybe the mightiest. Wilt thou not help me?" 🖋 "How can I help thee?" said the King, "thou who wilt not help thyself. Thou hast seen what thou shouldst do: do it then and be holpen" 🖋 Then said Hallblithe: "Wilt thou not slay me, O King, since thou wilt not do aught else?" 🖋 "Nay," said the King, "thy slaying wilt not serve me nor mine: I will neither help nor hinder. Thou art free to seek thy love wheresoever thou wilt in this my realm. Depart in peace!"

HALLBLITHE saw that the King was angry, tho' he smiled upon him; yet so coldly, that the face of him froze the very marrow of Hallblithe's bones: and he said within himself: "This King of lies shall not slay me, though mine anguish be hard to bear: for I am alive, and it may be that my love is in this land, & I may find her here, and how to reach another land I know not." So he turned from before the face of the King as the sun was setting, & he went down the land southward betwixt the mountains & the sea, not heeding whether it were night or day; and he went on till it was long past midnight, & then for mere weariness laid him down under a tree, not knowing where he was, and fell asleep.

AND in the morning he woke up to the bright sun, and found folk standing round about him, both men and women, and their sheep were anigh them, for they were shepherd folk. So when they saw that he was awake, they greeted him, and were blithe with him and made much of him; and they took him home to their house, and gave him to eat & to drink, and asked him what he would that they might serve him. And they seemed to him to be kind and simple folk, and though he loathed to speak the words, so sick at heart he was, yet he told them how he was seeking his troth-plight maiden, his earthly love, and asked them to say if they had seen any woman like her.

THEY heard him kindly and pitied him, and told him how they had heard of a woman in the land, who sought her beloved even as he sought his. And when he heard that, his heart leapt up, and he asked them to tell him more concerning this woman. Then they said that she dwelt in the hill-country in a goodly house, & had set her heart on a lovely man, whose image she had seen in a book, and that no man but this one would content her; and this, they said, was a sad and sorry matter, such as was unheard of hitherto in the land.

SO when Hallblithe heard this, as heavily as his heart fell again, he changed not countenance, but thanked the kind folk and departed, & went on down the land betwixt the mountains and the sea, and before nightfall he had been into three more houses of folk, and asked there of all comers concerning a woman who was sundered from her beloved; and at none of them gat he any answer to make him less sorry than yesterday. At the last of the three he slept, & on the morrow early there was the work to begin again; and the next day was the same as the last, and the day after differed not from it. Thus he went on seeking his beloved betwixt the mountains and the plain, till the great rock-wall came down to the side of the sea and made an end of the Glittering Plain on that side. Then he turned about and went back by the way that he had come, & up the country betwixt the mountains & the plain northward, until he had been into every house of folk in those parts and asked his question 🍂 Then he went up into that fair country of the dales, and even anigh to where dwelt the King's Daughter, and otherwhere in the land and everywhere, quartering the realm of the Glittering Plain as the heron quarters the flooded meadow when the waters draw aback into the river. So that now all people knew him when he came, and they wondered at him; but when he came to any house for the

third or fourth time, they wearied of him, and were glad
when he departed.

EVER it was one of two answers that he had: either
folk said to him, "There is no such woman; this land
is happy, and nought but happy people dwell herein;" or
else they told him of the woman who lived in sorrow, &
was ever looking on a book, that she might bring to her the
man whom she desired ✒ Whiles he wearied and longed
for death, but would not die until there was no corner of the
land unsearched. Whiles he shook off weariness, and went
about his quest as a craftsman sets about his work in the
morning. Whiles it irked him to see the soft and merry folk
of the land, who had no skill to help him, & he longed for the
house of his fathers & the men of the spear & the plough;
and thought: "Oh, if I might but get me back, if it were but
for an hour and to die there, to the meadows of the Raven,
and the acres beneath the mountains of Cleveland by the
Sea. Then at least should I learn some tale of what is or
what hath been, howsoever evil the tidings were, and not be
bandied about by lies for ever."

CHAPTER XV: YET HALLBLITHE SPEAKETH WITH THE KING.

O wore the days and the moons; & now were some six moons worn since first he came to the Glittering Plain; and he was come to Wood-end again, and heard and knew that the King was sitting once more in the door of his pavilion to hearken to the words of his people, and he said to himself: "I will speak yet again to this man, if indeed he be a man; yea, though he turn me into stone" 🍂 And he went up toward the pavilion; and on the way it came into his mind what the men of the kindred were doing that morning; & he had a vision of them as it were, and saw them yoking the oxen to the plough, and slowly going down the acres, as the shining iron drew the long furrow down the stubble-land, and the light haze hung about the elm-trees in the calm morning, & the smoke rose straight into the air from the roof of the kindred. And he said: "What is this? am I death-doomed this morning that this sight cometh so clearly upon me amidst the falseness of this unchanging land?"

THUS he came to the pavilion, and folk fell back before him to the right and the left, and he stood before the King, and said to him: "I cannot find her; she is not in thy land" 🍂 Then spake the King, smiling upon him, as erst: "What wilt thou then? Is it not time to rest?" 🍂 He said: "Yea, O King; but not in this land." Said the King: "Where else than in this land wilt thou find rest? Without is battle and famine, longing unsatisfied, and heart-burning and fear; within it is plenty and peace and good will and pleasure without cease. Thy word hath no meaning to me" 🍂 Saith Hallblithe: "Give me leave to depart, & I will bless thee" 🍂 "Is there nought else to do?" said the King. "Nought else," said Hallblithe 🍂 Therewith he felt that the King's face changed though he still smiled on him, and again he felt his heart grow cold before the King 🍂 But the King spake and said: "I hinder not thy departure, nor will any of my folk. No hand will be raised against thee; there is no weapon in all the land, save the deedless sword by my side & the weapons which thou bearest." Said Hallblithe: "Dost thou not owe me a joy in return for my beguiling?" 🍂 "Yea," said the King, "reach out thine hand to take it" 🍂 "One thing only may I take of thee," said Hallblithe; "my trothplight maiden or else the speeding of my departure" 🍂 Then said the King, & his voice was terrible though yet he smiled: "I will not hinder; I will not help. Depart in peace!"

WHEN Hallblithe turned away dizzy and half fainting, and strayed down the field, scarce knowing where he was; and as he went he felt his sleeve plucked at, and turned about, and lo! he was face to face with the Sea-eagle, no less joyous than aforetime. He took Hallblithe in his arms and embraced him and kissed him, and said: "Well met, faring-fellow! Whither away?" "Away out of this land of lies," said Hallblithe. The Sea-eagle shook his head, and quoth he: "Art thou still seeking a dream? And thou so fair that thou puttest all other men to shame" "I seek no dream," said Hallblithe, "but rather the end of dreams" "Well," said the Sea-eagle, "we will not wrangle about it. But hearken. Hard by in a pleasant nook of the meadows have I set up my tent; and although it be not as big as the King's pavilion, yet is it fair enough. Wilt thou not come thither with me and rest thee to-night; and to-morrow we will talk of this matter?"

NOW Hallblithe was weary and confused, and down-hearted beyond his wont, & the friendly words of the Sea-eagle softened his heart, and he smiled on him and said: "I give thee thanks; I will come with thee: thou art kind, & hast done nought to me save good from the time when I first saw thee lying in thy bed in the Hall of the Ravagers. Dost thou remember the day?" The Sea-eagle knitted his brow as one striving with a troublous memory, and said: "But dimly, friend, as if it had passed in an ugly dream: meseemeth my friendship with thee began when I came to thee from out of the wood, and saw thee standing with those three damsels; that I remember full well: ye were fair to look on" Hallblithe wondered at his words, but said no more about it, and they went together to a flow-ery nook nigh a stream of clear water where stood a silken tent, green like the grass which it stood on, & flecked with gold and goodly colours. Nigh it on the grass lay the

Sea-eagle's damsel, ruddy-cheeked and sweet-lipped, as fair
as aforetime. She turned about when she heard men coming, and when she saw Hallblithe a smile came into her
face like the sun breaking out on a fair but clouded morning, & she went up to him and took him by the hands and
kissed his cheek, and said: "Welcome, Spearman! welcome
back! We have heard of thee in many places, & have been
sorry that thou wert not glad, and now are we fain of thy
returning. Shall not sweet life begin for thee from henceforward?" 🖋 Again was Hallblithe moved by her kind welcome;
but he shook his head and spake: "Thou art kind, sister; yet
if thou wouldst be kinder thou wilt show me a way whereby
I may escape from this land. For abiding here has become
irksome to me, and meseemeth that hope is yet alive without the Glittering Plain." Her face fell as she answered:
"Yea, and fear also, and worse, if aught be worse. But come,
let us eat and drink in this fair place, and gather for thee a
little joyance before thou departest, if thou needs must
depart" 🖋 He smiled on her as one not ill-content, and laid
himself down on the grass, while the twain busied themselves, and brought forth fair cushions and a gilded table,
& laid dainty victual thereon and good wine.

S O they ate and drank together, and the Sea-eagle and
his mate became very joyous again, and Hallblithe
bestirred himself not to be a mar-feast; for he said within
himself: "I am departing, and after this time I shall see them
no more; and they are kind and blithe with me, and have
been aforetime; I will not make their merry hearts sore. For
when I am gone I shall be remembered of them but a little
while."

CHAPTER XVI: THOSE THREE GO THEIR WAYS TO THE EDGE OF THE GLITTERING PLAIN

S O the evening wore merrily; & they made Hallblithe lie in an ingle of the tent on a fair bed, and he was weary, & slept thereon like a child. But in the morning early they waked him; and while they were breaking their fast they began to speak to him of his departure, & asked him if he had an inkling of the way whereby he should get him gone, and he said: "If I escape it must needs be by the way of the mountains that wall the land about till they come down to the sea. For on the sea is no ship and no haven; and well I wot that no man of the land durst or can ferry me over to the land of my kindred, or otherwhere without the Glittering Plain. Tell me therefore (and I ask no more of you), is there any rumour or memory of a way that cleaveth yonder mighty wall of rock to other lands?" Said the damsel: "There is more than a memory or a rumour: there is a road through the mountains known to all men. For at whiles the earthly pilgrims come into the Glittering Plain thereby; and yet but seldom, so many are the griefs and perils which beset the wayfarers on that road. Whereof thou hadst far better bethink thee in time, and abide here and be happy with us & others who long sore to make thee happy" "Nay," said Hallblithe, "there is nought to do but tell me of the way, and I will depart at once, blessing you" Said the Sea-eagle: "More than that at least will we do. May I lose the bliss whereto I have attained, if I go not with thee to the very edge of the land of the Glittering Plain. Shall it not be so, sweetheart?" "Yea, at least we may do that," said the damsel; & she hung her head as if she were ashamed, and said: "And that is all that thou wilt get from us at most" Said Hallblithe: "It is enough, and I asked not so much." Then the damsel busied herself, and set meat and drink in two wallets, and took one herself and gave the other to the Sea-eagle, and said: "We will be thy porters, O Spearman, and will give thee a full wallet from the last house by the Desert of Dread, for when thou hast entered therein, thou mayst well find victual hard to come by: & now let us linger no more since the road is dear to thee."

SO they set forth on foot, for in that land men were slow to feel weariness; and turning about the hill of Woodend, they passed by some broken country, and came at even to a house at the entrance of a long valley, with high and steeply-sloping sides, which seemed, as it were, to cleave the dale country wherein they had fared aforetime. At that house they slept well-guested by its folk, and the next morning took their way down the valley, & the folk of the house stood at the door to watch their departure; for they had told the wayfarers that they had fared but a little way thitherward and knew of no folk who had used that road 🖋 So those three fared down the valley southward all day, ever mounting higher as they went. The way was pleasant and easy, for they went over fair, smooth, grassy lawns betwixt the hill-sides, beside a clear rattling stream that ran northward; at whiles were clumps of tall trees, oak for the most part, and at whiles thickets of thorn and eglantine and other such trees: so that they could rest well shaded when they would 🖋 They passed by no house of men, nor came to any such in the even, but lay down to sleep in a thicket of thorn and eglantine, and rested well, and on the morrow they rose up betimes and went on their ways 🖋 This second day as they went, the hill-sides on either hand grew lower, till at last they died out into a wide plain, beyond which in the southern offing the mountains rose huge and bare. This plain also was grassy and beset with trees and thickets here and there. Hereon they saw wild deer enough, as hart and buck, and roebuck and swine: withal a lion came out of a brake hard by them as they went, and stood gazing on them, so that Hallblithe looked to his weapons, and the Sea-eagle took up a big stone to fight with, being weaponless; but the damsel laughed, and tripped on her way lightly with girt-up gown, and the beast gave no more heed to them.

EASY and smooth was their way over this pleasant wilderness, & clear to see, though but little used, and before nightfall, after they had gone a long way, they came to a house. It was not large nor high, but was built very strongly and fairly of good ashlar: its door was shut, and on the jamb thereof hung a slug-horn. The damsel, who seemed to know what to do, set her mouth to the horn, and blew a blast; and in a little while the door was opened, and a big man clad in red scarlet stood therein: he had no weapons, but was somewhat surly of aspect: he spake not, but stood abiding the word: so the damsel took it up & said: "Art thou not the Warden of the Uttermost House?" 🖋 He said: "I am" 🖋 Said the damsel: "May we guest here to-night?" 🖋 He said: "The house lieth open to you with all that it hath of victual and plenishing: take what ye will, and use what ye will" 🖋 They thanked him; but he heeded not their thanks, and withdrew him from them. So they entered and found the table laid in a fair hall of stone carven & painted very goodly; so they ate and drank therein, and Hallblithe was of good heart, and the Sea-eagle and his mate were merry, though they looked softly and shyly on Hallblithe because of the sundering anigh; and they saw no man in the house save the man in scarlet, who went and came about his business, pay-ing no heed to them. So when the night was deep they lay down in the shut-bed off the hall, and slept, & the hours were tidingless to them until they woke in the morning.

ON the morrow they arose & broke their fast, and there-after the damsel spake to the man in scarlet and said: "May we fill our wallets with victual for the way?" 🖋 Said the Warden: "There lieth the meat" 🖋 So they filled their wallets, while the man looked on; and they came to the door when they were ready, and he unlocked it to them, saying no word. But when they turned their faces towards the moun-tains he spake at last, and stayed them at the first step. Quoth he: "Whither away? Ye take the wrong road!" 🖋 Said Hallblithe: "Nay, for we go toward the mountains and the edge of the Glittering Plain" 🖋 "Ye shall do ill to go thither," said the Warden, "and I bid you forbear" 🖋 "O Warden of the Uttermost House, wherefore should we forbear?" said the Sea-eagle 🖋 Said the scarlet man: "Because my charge is to further those who would go inward to the King, and to stay those who would go outward from the King" 🖋 "How then if we go outward despite thy bidding?" said the Sea-eagle, "wilt thou then hinder us perforce?" 🖋 "How may I," said the man, "since thy fellow hath weapons?" 🖋 "Go we forth, then," said the Sea-eagle 🖋 "Yea," said the damsel, "we will go forth. And know, O Warden, that this weaponed man only

is of mind to fare over the edge of the Glittering Plain; but
we twain shall come back hither again, & fare inwards" 🖋
Said the Warden: "Nought is it to me what ye will do when
ye are past this house. Nor shall any man who goeth out of
this garth toward the mountains ever come back inwards
save he cometh in the company of new comers to the Glittering Plain" 🖋 "Who shall hinder him?" said the Sea-eagle.
"The KING," said the Warden 🖋 Then there was silence
awhile, and the man said: "Now do as ye will." And therewith he turned back into the house & shut the door.

BUT the Sea-eagle & the damsel stood gazing on one
another, and at Hallblithe; and the damsel was downcast and pale; but the Sea-eagle cried out: "Forward now, O
Hallblithe, since thou willest it, and we will go with thee and
share whatever may befall thee; yea, right up to the very
edge of the Glittering Plain. And thou, O beloved, why dost
thou delay? Why dost thou stand as if thy fair feet were
grown to the grass?"

BUT the damsel gave a lamentable cry, & cast herself
down on the ground, & knelt before the Sea-eagle, and
took him by the knees, and said betwixt sobbing and weeping: "O my lord and love, I pray thee to forbear, and the
Spearman, our friend, shall pardon us. For if thou goest, I
shall never see thee more, since my heart will not serve me
to go with thee. O forbear! I pray thee!" 🖋 And she grovelled on the earth before him; and the Sea-eagle waxed red,
and would have spoken but Hallblithe cut his speech across,
and said "Friends, be at peace! For this is the minute that
sunders us. Get ye back at once to the heart of the Glittering Plain, and live there and be happy; and take my blessing
and thanks for the love and help that ye have given me. For
your going forward with me should destroy you and profit
me nothing. It would be but as the host bringing his guests
one field beyond his garth, when their goal is the ends of the
earth; and if there were a lion in the path, why should he
perish for courtesy's sake?" 🖋 Therewith he stooped down

to the damsel, and lifted her up & kissed her face; and he
cast his arms about the Sea-eagle & said to him: "Farewell,
shipmate!" 🍃 Then the damsel gave him the wallet of victual, and bade him farewell, weeping sorely; and he looked
kindly on them for a moment of time, & then turned away
from them and fared on toward the mountains, striding with
great strides, holding his head aloft. But they looked no more
on him, having no will to eke their sorrow, but went their
ways back again without delay.

CHAPTER XVII: HALLBLITHE AMONGST THE MOUNTAINS

S O strode on Hallblithe; but when he had gone but a little way his head turned, and the earth and heavens wavered before him, so that he must needs sit down on

a stone by the wayside, wondering what ailed him ✿ Then
he looked up at the mountains, which now seemed quite near
to him at the plain's ending, and his weakness increased on
him; and lo! as he looked, it was to him as if the crags rose
up in the sky to meet him and overhang him, and as if the
earth heaved up beneath him, and therewith he fell aback &
lost all sense, so that he knew not what was become of the
earth and the heavens & the passing of the minutes of
his life.

WHEN he came to himself he knew not whether he
had lain so a great while or a little; he felt feeble,
and for a while he lay scarce moving, and beholding nought, not even the sky above him. Presently
he turned about and saw hard stone on either side, so he
rose wearily and stood upon his feet, and knew that he was
faint with hunger and thirst. Then he looked around him,
and saw that he was in a narrow valley or cleft of the mountains amidst wan rocks, bare and waterless, where grew no
blade of green; but he could see no further than the sides
of that cleft, and he longed to be out of it that he might see
whitherward to turn. Then he bethought him of his wallet,
and set his hand to it and opened it, thinking to get victual
thence; but lo! it was all spoilt and wasted. None the less, for
all his feebleness, he turned and went toiling slowly along
what seemed to be a path little trodden leading upward out
of the cleft; and at last he reached the crest thereof, and sat
him down on a rock on the other side; yet durst not raise his
eyes awhile and look on the land, lest he should see death
manifest therein. At last he looked, and saw that he was
high up amongst the mountain-peaks: before him and on
either hand was but a world of fallow stone rising ridge upon
ridge like the waves of the wildest of the winter sea. The sun
not far from its midmost shone down bright & hot on that
wilderness; yet was there no sign that any man had ever
been there since the beginning of the world, save that the
path aforesaid seemed to lead onward down the stony slope.

THIS way & that way and all about he gazed, straining his eyes if perchance he might see any diversity in the stony waste; and at last betwixt two peaks of the rock-wall on his left hand he descried a streak of green mingling with the cold blue of the distance; & he thought in his heart that this was the last he should see of the Glittering Plain. Then he spake aloud in that desert, and said, though there was none to hear: "Now is my last hour come; and here is Hallblithe of the Raven perishing, with his deeds undone and his longing unfulfilled, & his bridal-bed a-cold for ever. Long may the House of the Raven abide & flourish, with many a man and maiden, valiant and fruitful! O kindred, cast thy blessing on this man about to die here, doing none otherwise than ye would have him!"

HE sat there a little while longer, and then he said to himself: "Death tarries; were it not well that I go to meet him, even as the cot-carle preventeth the mighty chieftain?" Then he arose, and went painfully down the slope, steadying himself with the shaft of his gleaming spear; but all at once he stopped; for it seemed to him that he heard voices borne on the wind that blew up the mountain-side. But he shook his head and said: "Now forsooth beginneth the dream which shall last for ever; nowise am I beguiled by it." None the less he strove the more eagerly with the wind & the way and his feebleness; yet did the weakness wax on him, so that it was but a little while ere he faltered and reeled and fell down once more in a swoon.

WHEN he came to himself again he was no longer alone: a man was kneeling down by him and holding up his head, while another before him, as he opened his eyes, put a cup of wine to his lips. So Hallblithe drank and was refreshed; and presently they gave him bread, and he ate, & his heart was strengthened, and the happiness of life returned to it, and he lay back, and slept sweetly for a season.

HEN he awoke from that slumber he found that he had gotten back much of his strength again, and he sat up and looked around him, & saw three men sitting anigh, armed & girt with swords, yet in evil array, and sore travel-worn. One of these was very old, with long white hair hanging down; and another, though he was not so much stricken in years, still looked an old man of over sixty winters. The third was a man some forty years old, but sad and sorry & drooping of aspect 🍃 So when they saw him stirring, they all fixed their eyes upon him, and the oldest man said: "Welcome to him who erst had no tidings for us!" And the second said: "Tell us now thy tidings." But the third, the sorry man, cried out aloud, saying: "Where is the land? Where is the land?" Said Hallblithe: "Meseemeth the land which ye seek is the land which I seek to flee from. And now I will not hide that meseemeth I have seen you before, & that was at Cleveland by the Sea when the days were happier" 🍃 Then they all three bowed their heads in yea-say, and spake: '"Where is the land? Where is the land?" Then Hallblithe arose to his feet, & said: "Ye have healed me of the sickness of death, and I will do what I may to heal you of your sickness of sorrow. Come up the pass with me, and I will show you the land afar off" 🍃 Then they arose like young and brisk men, and he led them over the brow of the ridge into the little valley wherein he had first come to himself: there he showed them that glimpse of a green land betwixt the two peaks, which he had beheld e'en now; and they stood a while looking at it and weeping for joy 🍃 Then spake the oldest of the seekers: "Show us the way to the land" 🍃 "Nay," said Hallblithe, "I may not; for when I would depart thence, I might not go by mine own will, but was borne out hither, I wot not how. For when I came to the edge of the land against the will of the King, he smote me, and then cast me out. Therefore since I may not help you, find ye the land for yourselves, & let me go blessing you, and come out of this desert by the way whereby ye entered it. For I have an errand in the world."

SPAKE the youngest of the seekers: "Now art thou become the yoke-fellow of Sorrow, & thou must wend, not whither thou wouldst, but whither she will: & she would have thee go forward toward life, not backward toward death."

SAID the midmost seeker: "If we let thee go further into the wilderness thou shalt surely die: for hence to the peopled parts, and the City of Merchants, whence we come, is a month's journey: & there is neither meat nor drink, nor beast nor bird, nor any green thing all that way; and since we have found thee famishing, we may well deem that thou hast no victual. As to us we have but little; so that if it be much more than three days' journey to the Glittering Plain, we may well starve and die within sight of the Acre of the Undying. Nevertheless that little will we share with thee if thou wilt help us to find that good land; so that thou mayst yet put away Sorrow, and take Joy again to thy board and bed."

HALLBLITHE hung his head and answered nought; for he was confused by the meshes of ill-hap, and his soul grew sick with the bitterness of death. But the sad man spake again and said: "Thou hast an errand sayest thou? is it such as a dead man may do?" 🖋 Hallblithe pondered, and amidst the anguish of his despair was borne in on him a vision of the sea-waves lapping the side of a black ship, and a man therein: who but himself, set free to do his errand, and his heart was quickened within him, & he said: "I thank you, and I will wend back with you, since there is no road for me save back again into the trap" 🖋 The three seekers seemed glad thereat, & the second one said: "Though death is pursuing, and life lieth ahead, yet will we not hasten thee unduly. Time was when I was Captain of the Host, & learned how battles were lost by lack of rest. Therefore have thy sleep now, that thou mayst wax in strength for our helping" 🖋 Said Hallblithe: "I need not rest; I may not rest; I will not rest" 🖋 Said the sad man: "It is lawful for thee to rest. So say I, who was once a master of law" 🌿 Said the long-hoary elder: "And I command thee to rest; I who was once the king of a mighty folk."

IN sooth Hallblithe was now exceeding weary; so he laid him down and slept sweetly in the stony wilderness amidst those three seekers, the old, the sad, and the very old.

WHEN he awoke he felt well and strong again, and he leapt to his feet & looked about him, and saw the three seekers stirring, and he deemed by the sun that it was early morning. The sad man brought forth bread and water & wine, and they broke their fast; and when they had done he spake & said: "Abideth now in wallet and bottle but one more full meal for us, & then no more save a few crumbs and a drop or two of wine if we husband it well" 🌿 Said the second elder: "Get we to the road, then, and make haste. I have been seeking, and meseemeth, though the way be long, it is not utterly blind for us. Or look thou, Raven-son, is there not a path yonder that leadeth onward up to the brow of the ghyll again? & as I have seen, it leadeth on again down from the said brow."

FORSOOTH there was a track that led through the stony tangle of the wilderness; so they took to the road with a good heart, and went all day, and saw no living thing, and not a blade of grass or a trickle of water: nought save the wan rocks under the sun; and though they trusted in their road that it led them aright, they saw no other glimpse of the Glittering Plain, because there rose a great ridge like a wall on the north side, and they went as it were down along a trench of the rocks, albeit it was whiles broken across by ghylls, and knolls, and reefs.

SO at sunset they rested and ate their victual, for they were very weary; and thereafter they lay down, & slept as soundly as if they were in the best of the halls of men. On the morrow betimes they arose soberly and went their ways with few words, and, as they deemed, the path still led them onward. And now the great ridge on the north rose steeper and steeper, and their crossing it seemed not to be thought of; but their half-blind track failed them not. They rested at even, and ate & drank what little they had left, save a mouthful or two of wine, and then went on again by the light of the moon, which was so bright that they still saw their way. And it happened to Hallblithe, as mostly it does with men very travel-worn, that he went on and on scarce remembering where he was, or who his fellows were, or that he had any fellows 🍃 So at midnight they lay down in the wilderness again, hungry and weary. They rose at dawn and went forward with waning hope: for now the mountain ridge on the north was close to their path, rising up along a sheer wall of pale stone over which nothing might go save the fowl flying; so that at first on that morning they looked for nought save to lay their bones in that grievous desert where no man should find them. But, as beset with famine, they fared on heavily down the narrow track, there came a hoarse cry from Hallblithe's dry throat and it was as if his cry had been answered by another like to his; & the seekers turned and beheld him pointing to the cliff-side, & lo! half-way up the pale sun-litten crag stood two ravens in a cranny of the stone, flapping their wings & croaking, with thrusting forth & twisting of their heads; and presently they came floating on the thin pure air high up over the heads of the wayfarers, croaking for the pleasure of the meeting, as though they laughed thereat.

THEN rose the heart of Hallblithe, & he smote his palms together, & fell to singing an old song of his people, amidst the rocks whereas few men had sung aforetime.

WHENCE are ye and whither,
O fowl of our fathers?

What field have ye looked on,
what acres unshorn?
What land have ye left
where the battle-folk gathers,
And the war-helms are white
o'er the paths of the corn?

WHAT tale do ye bear
of the people uncraven,
Where amidst the long hall-
shadow sparkle the spears;
Where aloft on the hall-ridge
now flappeth the raven,
And singeth the song
of the nourishing years?

THERE gather the lads
in the first of the morning,
While white lies the battle-
day's dew on the grass,
And the kind steeds trot up
to the horn's voice of warning,
And the winds wake and whine
in the dusk of the pass.

O FOWL of our fathers,
why now are ye resting?
Come over the mountains
and look on the foe.
Full fair after fight won
shall yet be your nesting;
And your fledglings
the sons of the kindred shall know.

Therewith he strode with his head upraised, and above him
flew the ravens, croaking as if they answered his song in
friendly fashion.

IT was but a little after this that the path turned aside sharp toward the cliffs, and the seekers were abashed thereof, till Hallblithe running forward beheld a great cavern in the face of the cliff at the path's ending: so he turned and cried on his fellows, and they hastened up, and presently stood before that cavern's mouth with doubt & joy mingled in their minds; for now, mayhappen, they had reached the gate of the Glittering Plain, or mayhappen the gate of death 🍂 The sad man hung his head and spake: "Doth not some new trap abide us? What do we here? is this aught save death?" Spake the Elder of Elders: "Was not death on either hand e'en now, even as treason besetteth the king upon his throne?" 🍂 And the second said: "Yea, we were as the host which hath no road save through the multitude of foemen" 🍂 But Hallblithe laughed & said: "Why do ye hang back, then? As for me, if death be here, soon is mine errand sped" 🍂 Therewith he led the way into the dark of the cave, and the ravens hung about the crag overhead croaking, as the men left the light. So was their way swallowed up in the cavern, and day and its time became nought to them; they went on and on, and became exceeding faint and weary, but rested not, for death was behind them. Whiles they deemed they heard waters running, & whiles the singing of fowl; and to Hallblithe it seemed that he heard his name called, so that he shouted back in answer; but all was still when the sound of his voice had died out.

AT last, when they were pressing on again after a short while of resting, Hallblithe cried out that the cave was lightening: so they hastened onward, and the light grew till they could see each other, & dimly they beheld the cave that it was both wide and high. Yet a little further, & their faces showed white to one another, & they could see the crannies of the rocks, and the bats hanging garlanded from the roof. So then they came to where the day streamed down bright on them from a break overhead, and lo! the sky & green leaves waving against it.

TO those way-worn men it seemed hard to clamber out that way, & especially to the elders: so they went on a little further to see if there were aught better abiding them, but when they found the daylight failing them again, they turned back to the place of the break in the roof, lest they should waste their strength and perish in the bowels of the mountain. So with much ado they hove up Hallblithe till he got him first on to a ledge of the rocky wall, and so, what by strength, what by cunning, into the daylight through the rent in the roof. So when he was without he made a rope of his girdle & strips from his raiment, for he was ever a deft craftsman, and made a shift to heave up therewith the sad man, who was light and lithe of body; and then the two together dealt with the Elders one after another, till they were all four on the face of the earth again ✤ The place whereto they had gotten was the side of a huge mountain, stony and steep, but set about with bushes, which seemed full fair to those wanderers amongst the rocks ✤ This mountain-slope went down towards a fair green plain, which Hallblithe made no doubt was the outlying waste of the Glittering Plain: nay, he deemed that he could see afar off thereon the white walls of the Uttermost House. So much he told the seekers in few words; and then while they grovelled on the earth and wept for pure joy, whereas the sun was down and it was beginning to grow dusk, he went and looked around soberly to see if he might find water and any kind of victual; and presently a little down the hillside he came upon a place where a spring came gushing up out of the earth and ran down toward the plain; and about it was green grass growing plentifully, and a little thicket of bramble and wilding fruit-trees. So he drank of the water, & plucked him a few wilding apples somewhat better than crabs, and then went up the hill again & fetched the seekers to that mountain hostelry; and while they drank of the stream he plucked them apples & bramble-berries. For indeed they were as men out of their wits, and were dazed by the extremity of their joy, and as men long shut up in prison, to whom the world of men-folk hath become strange. Simple as the victual was,

they were somewhat strengthened by it and by the plentiful
water, and as night was now upon them, it was of no avail
for them to go further: so they slept beneath the boughs of
the thorn-bushes.

CHAPTER XVIII: HALLBLITHE DWELLETH IN THE WOOD ALONE 🌸🌸

UT on the morrow they arose betimes, & broke their fast on that woodland victual, and then went speedily down the mountain-side; and Hallblithe saw by the clear morning light that it was indeed the Uttermost House which he had seen across the green waste. So he told the seekers; but they were silent & heeded nought, because of a fear that had come upon them, lest they should die before they came into that good land. At the foot of the mountain they came upon a river, deep but not wide, with low grassy banks, and Hallblithe, who was an exceeding strong swimmer, helped the seekers over without much ado; and there they stood upon the grass of that goodly waste. Hallblithe looked on them to note if any change should come over them, and he deemed that already they were become stronger and of more avail. But he spake nought thereof, and strode on toward the Uttermost House, even as that other day he had stridden away from it. Such diligence they made, that it was but little after noon when they came to the door thereof. Then Hallblithe took the horn and blew upon it, while his fellows stood by murmuring, "It is the Land! It is the Land!"

SO came the Warden to the door, clad in red scarlet, & the elder went up to him and said: "Is this the Land?" "What land?" said the Warden "Is it the Glittering Plain?" said the second of the seekers "Yea, forsooth," said the Warden. Said the sad man: "Will ye lead us to the King? "Ye shall come to the King," said the Warden "When, oh when?" cried they out all three "The morrow of to-morrow, maybe," said the Warden "Oh! if to-morrow were but come!" they cried "It will come," said the red man; "enter ye the house, and eat and drink and rest you." So they entered, and the Warden heeded Hallblithe nothing. They ate and drank and then went to their rest, and Hallblithe lay in a shut-bed off from the hall, but the Warden brought the seekers otherwhere, so that Hallblithe saw them not after he had gone to bed; but as for him he slept and forgot that aught was.

IN the morning when he awoke he felt very strong and well-liking; & he beheld his limbs that they were clear of skin and sleek and fair; and he heard one hard by in the hall carolling and singing joyously. So he sprang from his

bed with the wonder of sleep yet in him, and drew the cur-
tains of the shut-bed and looked forth into the hall; and lo!
on the high-seat a man of thirty winters by seeming, tall,
fair of fashion, with golden hair and eyes as grey as glass,
proud and noble of aspect; and anigh him sat another man of
like age to look on, a man strong & burly, with short curling
brown hair and a red beard, and ruddy countenance, & the
mien of a warrior. Also, up and down the hall, paced a man
younger of aspect than these two, tall and slender, black-
haired & dark-eyed, amorous of countenance; he it was who
was singing a snatch of song as he went lightly on the hall
pavement: a snatch like to this:

FAIR is the world, now autumn's wearing,
And the sluggard sun lies long abed;
Sweet are the days, now winter's nearing,
And all winds feign that the wind is dead.

Dumb is the hedge where the crabs hang yellow,
Bright as the blossoms of the spring;
Dumb is the close where the pears grow mellow,
And none but the dauntless redbreasts sing.

Fair was the spring, but amidst his greening
Grey were the days of the hidden sun;
Fair was the summer, but overweening,
So soon his o'er-sweet days were done.

Come then, love, for peace is upon us,
Far off is failing, and far is fear,
Here where the rest in the end hath won us,
In the garnering tide of the happy year.

Come from the grey old house by the water,
Where, far from the lips of the hungry sea,
Green groweth the grass o'er the field of the slaughter,
And all is a tale for thee and me.

SO Hallblithe did on his raiment & went into the hall; and when those three saw him they smiled upon him kindly and greeted him; and the noble man at the board said: "Thanks have thou, O Warrior of the Raven, for thy help in our need: thy reward from us shall not be lacking" 🍃 Then the brown-haired man came up to him, & clapped him on the back and said to him: "Brisk man of the Raven, good is thy help at need; even so shall be mine to thee henceforward" 🍃 But the young man stepped up to him lightly, and cast his arms about him, and kissed him, and said: "O friend & fellow, who knoweth but I may one day help thee as thou hast holpen me? though thou art one who by seeming mayst well help thyself. And now mayst thou be as merry as I am to-day!" 🍃 Then they all three cried out joyously: "It is the Land! It is the Land!" 🍃 So Hallblithe knew that these men were the two elders and the sad man of yesterday, and that they had renewed their youth.

JOYOUSLY now did those men break their fast: nor did Hallblithe make any grim countenance, for he thought: "That which these dotards and drivellers have been mighty enough to find, shall I not be mighty enough to flee from?" Breakfast done, the seekers made little delay, so eager as they were to behold the King, and to have handsel of their new sweet life. So they got them ready to depart, and the once-captain said: "Art thou able to lead us to the King, O Raven-son, or must we seek another man to do so much for us?" Said Hallblithe: "I am able to lead you so nigh unto Wood-end (where, as I deem, the King abideth) that ye shall not miss him." Therewith they went to the door, & the Warden unlocked to them, and spake no word to them when they departed, though they thanked him kindly for the guesting.

WHEN they were without the garth, the young man fell to running about the meadow plucking great handfuls of the rich flowers that grew about, singing and carolling the while. But he who had been king looked up & down and round about, and said at last: "Where be the horses and the men?" But his fellow with the red beard said: "Raven-son, in this land when they journey, what do they as to riding or going afoot?" Said Hallblithe: "Fair fellows, ye shall wot that in this land folk go afoot for the most part, both men and women; whereas they weary but little, and are in no haste" 🍂 Then the once-captain clapped the once-king on the shoulder, and said: "Hearken, lord, and delay no longer, but gird up thy gown, since here is no mare's son to help thee: for fair is to-day that lies before us, with many a fair new day beyond it."

SO Hallblithe led the way inward, thinking of many things, yet but little of his fellows. Albeit they, and the younger man especially, were of many words; for this black-haired man had many questions to ask, chiefly concerning the women, what they were like to look on, and of what mood they were. Hallblithe answered thereto as long as he might, but at last he laughed and said: "Friend, forbear thy questions now; for meseemeth in a few hours thou shalt be as wise hereon as is the God of Love himself."

SO they made diligence along the road, and all was tidingless till on the second day at even they came to the first house off the waste. There had they good welcome, and slept. But on the morrow when they arose, Hallblithe spake to the Seekers, and said: "Now are things much changed betwixt us since the time when we first met: for then I had all my desire, as I thought, and ye had but one desire, and well-nigh lacked hope of its fulfilment. Whereas now the lack hath left you and come to me. Wherefore even as time agone ye might not abide even one night at the House of the Raven, so hard as your desire lay on you; even so it fareth with me to-day, that I am consumed with my desire, and I may not abide with you; lest that befall which befalleth betwixt the full man and the fasting. Wherefore now I bless you and depart."

THEY abounded in words of good-will to him, & the once-king said: "Abide with us, and we shall see to it that thou have all the dignities that a man may think of" 🍃 And the once-captain said: "Lo, here is mine hand that hath been mighty; never shalt thou lack it for the accomplishment of thine uttermost desire. Abide with us" 🍃 Lastly said the young man: "Abide with us, Son of the Raven! Set thine heart on a fair woman, yea even were it the fairest; & I will get her for thee, even were my desire set on her" 🍃 But he smiled on them, and shook his head, and said: "All hail to you! but mine errand is yet undone." And therewith he departed.

HE skirted Wood-end and came not to it, but got him down to the side of the sea, not far from where he first came aland, but somewhat south of it. A fair oak-wood came down close to the beach of the sea; it was some four miles end-long & over-thwart. Thither Hallblithe betook him, and in a day or two got him wood-wright's tools from a house of men a little outside the wood, three miles from the sea-shore. Then he set to work and built him a little frame-house on a lawn of the wood beside a clear stream; for he was a very deft wood-wright. Withal he made him a bow and arrows, and shot what he would of the fowl and the deer for his livelihood; and folk from that house and otherwhence came to see him, and brought him bread & wine and spicery and other matters which he needed. And the days wore, & men got used to him, and loved him as if he had been a rare image which had been brought to that land for its adornment; & now they no longer called him the Spearman, but the Wood-lover. And as for him, he took all in patience, abiding what the lapse of days should bring forth.

CHAPTER XIX: HALLBLITHE BUILDS HIM A SKIFF ✿✿

FTER Hallblithe had been housed a little while, & the time was again drawing nigh to the twelfth moon since he had come to the Glittering Plain, he went in the wood one day; and, pondering many things without fixing on any one, he stood before a very great oak-tree and looked at the tall straight bole thereof, and there came into his head the words of an old song which was written round a scroll of the carving over the shut-bed, wherein he was wont to lie when he was at home in the House of the Raven: and thus it said:

I AM the oak-tree, and forsooth
Men deal by me with little ruth;
My boughs they shred, my life they slay,
And speed me o'er the watery way.

He looked up into that leafy world for a little and then turned back toward his house; but all day long, whether he were at work or at rest, that posy ran in his head, and he kept on saying it over, aloud or not aloud, till the day was done and he went to sleep.

THEN in his sleep he dreamed that an exceeding fair woman stood by his bedside, and at first she seemed to him to be an image of the Hostage. But presently her face changed, and her body and her raiment; and, lo! it was the lovely woman, the King's daughter whom he had seen wasting her heart for the love of him. Then even in his dream shame thereof overtook him, and because of that shame he awoke, and lay awake a little, hearkening the wind going through the woodland boughs, and the singing of the owl who had her dwelling in the hollow oak nigh to his house. Slumber overcame him in a little while, & again the image of the King's daughter came to him in his dream, and again when he looked upon her, shame and pity rose so hotly in his heart that he awoke weeping, & lay a while hearkening to the noises of the night. The third time he slept and dreamed; and once more that image came to him. And now he looked, and saw that she had in her hand a book covered outside with gold & gems, even as he saw it in the orchard-close aforetime: and he beheld her face that it was no longer the face of one sick with sorrow; but glad and clear, and most beauteous.

NOW she opened the book and held it before Hallblithe and turned the leaves so that he might see them clearly; & therein were woods and castles painted, & burning mountains, and the wall of the world, and kings upon their thrones, and fair women and warriors, all most lovely to behold, even as he had seen it aforetime in the orchard when he lay lurking amidst the leaves of the bay-tree.

SO at last she came to the place in the book wherein was painted Hallblithe's own image over against the image of the Hostage; and he looked thereon & longed. But she turned the leaf, and, lo! on one side the Hostage again, standing in a fair garden of the spring with the lilies all about her feet, and behind her the walls of a house, grey, ancient, & lovely: and on the other leaf over against her was painted a sea rippled by a little wind and a boat thereon sailing swiftly, and one man alone in the boat sitting & steering with a cheerful countenance; and he, who but Hallblithe himself. Hallblithe looked thereon for a while & then the King's daughter shut the book, and the dream flowed into other imaginings of no import.

IN the grey dawn Hallblithe awoke, & called to mind his dream, & he leapt from his bed and washed the night from off him in the stream, and clad himself and went the shortest way through the wood to that House of folk aforesaid: and as he went his face was bright & he sang the second part of the carven posy; to wit:

ALONG the grass I lie forlorn
That when a while of time is worn,
I may be filled with war and peace
And bridge the sundering of the seas.

HE came out of the wood and hastened over the flowery meads of the Glittering Plain, and came to that same house when it was yet very early. At the door he came across a damsel bearing water from the well, and she spake to him and said: "Welcome, Wood-lover! Seldom art thou seen in our garth; & that is a pity of thee. And now I look on thy face I see that gladness hath come into thine heart, and that thou art most fair and lovely. Here then is a token for thee of the increase of gladness." Therewith she set her buckets on the earth, and stood before him, and took him by the ears, and drew down his face to hers and kissed him sweetly. He smiled on her & said: "I thank thee, sister, for the kiss and the greeting; but I come here having a lack" 🍂 "Tell us," she said, "that we may do thee a pleasure" 🍂 He said: "I would ask the folk to give me timber, both beams and battens and boards; for if I hew in the wood it will take long to season" 🍂 "All this is free for thee to take from our wood-store when thou hast broken thy fast with us," said the damsel. "Come thou in and rest thee."

SHE took him by the hand and they went in together, and she gave him to eat and drink, and went up and down the house, saying to every one: "Here is come the Wood-lover, and he is glad again; come & see him" 🍂 So the folk gathered about him, and made much of him. And when they had made an end of breakfast, the head man of the House said to him: "The beasts are in the wain, and the timber abideth thy choosing; come and see." So he brought Hallblithe to the timber-bower, where he chose for himself all that he needed of oak-timber of the best; and they loaded the wain therewith, & gave him what he would moreover of nails and tree-nails and other matters; and he thanked them; and they said to him: "Whither now shall we lead thy timber?" 🍂 "Down to the sea-side," quoth he, "nighest to my dwelling" 🍂 So did they, & more than a score, men and women, went with him, some in the wain, and some afoot. Thus they came down to the sea-shore, and laid the timber on the strand just above high-water mark; and straightway Hallblithe fell to work shaping him a boat, for well he knew the whole craft thereof; and the folk looked on wondering, till the tide had ebbed the little it was wont to ebb, and left the moist sand firm and smooth; then the women left watching Hallblithe's work, & fell to paddling barefoot in the clear water, for there was scarce a ripple on the sea; and the carles came and played with them so that Hallblithe was left alone a while; for this kind of play was new to that folk, since they seldom came down to the sea-side. Thereafter they needs must dance together, & would have had Hallblithe dance with them; and when he naysaid them because he was fain of his work, in all playfulness they fell to taking the adze out of his hand, whereat he became somewhat wroth, and they were afraid and went and had their dance out without him.

BY this time the sun was grown very hot, and they came to him again, and lay down about him & watched his work, for they were weary. And one of the women, still panting with the dance, spake as she looked on the loveliness of her limbs, which one of the swains was caressing: "Brother," said she, "great strokes thou smitest; when wilt thou have smitten the last of them, and come to our house again?" 🍃 "Not for many days, fair sister," said he, without looking up 🍃 "Alas that thou shouldst talk so," said a carle, rising up from the warm sand; "what shall all thy toil win thee?" 🍃 Spake Hallblithe: "Maybe a merry heart, or maybe death."

AT that word they all rose up together, and stood huddled together like sheep that have been driven to the croft-gate, and the shepherd hath left them for a little and they know not whither to go. Little by little they got them to the wain and harnessed their beasts thereto, & departed silently by the way that they had come; but in a little time Hallblithe heard their laughter & merry speech across the flowery meadows. He heeded their departure little, but went on working, and worked the sun down, and on till the stars began to twinkle. Then he went home to his house in the wood, & slept and dreamed not, and began again on the morrow with a good heart.

O be short, no day passed that he wrought not his full tale of work, and the days wore, and his ship-wright's work throve. Often the folk of that house, and from otherwhere round about, came down to the strand to watch him working. Nowise did they wilfully hinder him, but whiles when they could get no talk from him, they would speak of him to each other, wondering that he should so toil to sail upon the sea; for they loved the sea but little, and it soon became clear to them that he was look-ing to nought else: though it may not be said that they deemed he would leave the land for ever. On the other hand, if they hindered him not, neither did they help, saving when he prayed them for somewhat which he needed, which they would then give him blithely.

F the Sea-eagle and his damsel, Hallblithe saw nought; whereat he was well content, for he deemed it of no avail to make a second sundering of it ✿ So he worked and kept his heart up, & at last all was ready; he had made him a mast and a sail, and oars, and whatso-other gear there was need of. So then he thrust his skiff into the sea on an even-ing whenas there were but two carles standing by; for there would often be a score or two of folk. These two smiled on him and bespake him kindly, but would not help him when he bade them set shoulder to her bows and shove. Albeit he got the skiff into the water without much ado, and got into her, and brought her to where a stream running from out of his wood made a little haven for her up from the sea. There he tied her to a tree-bole, and busied himself that even with getting the gear into her, & victual & water withal, as much as he deemed he should need: and so, being weary, he went to his house to sleep, thinking that he should awake in the grey of the morning & thrust out into the deep sea. And he was the more content to abide, because on that eve, as ofte-nest betid, the wind blew landward from the sea, whereas in the morning it oftenest blew seaward from the land. In any case he thought to be astir so timely that he should come alone to his keel, and depart with no leave-takings. But, as

it fell out, he overslept himself, so that when he came out
into the wood clad in all his armour, with his sword girt to
his side, & his spear over his shoulder, he heard the voices of
folk, and presently found so many gathered about his boat
that he had some ado to get aboard.

THE folk had brought many gifts for him of such things
as they deemed he might need for a short voyage, as
fruit and wine, and woollen cloths to keep the cold night
from him; he thanked them kindly as he stepped over the
gunwale, and some of the women kissed him: and one said
(she it was, who had met him at the stead that morning
when he went to fetch timber): "Thou wilt be back this
even, wilt thou not, brother? It is yet but early, & thou
shalt have time enough to take all thy pleasure on the sea,
and then come back to us to eat thy meat in our house at
nightfall."

SHE spake, knitting her brows in longing for his return;
but he knew that all those deemed he would come back
again soon; else had they deemed him a rebel of the King,
and might, as he thought, have stayed him. So he changed
not countenance in any wise, but said only: "farewell, sister,
for this day, & farewell to all you till I come back." Therewith
he unmoored his boat, & sat down and took the oars, and
rowed till he was out of the little haven, and on the green
sea, and the keel rose and fell on the waves. Then he stepped
the mast and hoisted sail, & sheeted home, for the morning
wind was blowing gently from the mountains over the meadows of the Glittering Plain, so the sail filled, and the keel
leapt forward and sped over the face of the cold sea. And it
is to be said that whether he wotted or not, it was the very
day twelve months since he had come to that shore along
with the Sea-eagle. So that folk stood and watched the skiff
growing less and less upon the deep till they could scarce see
her. Then they turned about and went into the wood to dis-
port them, for the sun was growing hot. Nevertheless, there
were some of them (and that damsel was one), who came

back to the sea-shore from time to time all day long; & even when the sun was down they looked seaward under the rising moon, expecting to see Hallblithe's bark come into the shining path which she drew across the waters round about the Glittering Plain.

CHAPTER XX: SO NOW SAILETH HALLBLITHE AWAY FROM THE GLITTERING PLAIN

BUT as to Hallblithe, he soon lost sight of the Glittering Plain and the mountains thereof, and there was nought but sea all round about him, and his heart filled with joy as he sniffed the brine and watched the gleaming hills and valleys of the restless deep; & he said to himself that he was going home to his Kindred and the Roof of his Fathers of old time 🍂 He stood as near due north as he might; but as the day wore, the wind headed him, and he deemed it not well to beat, lest he should make his voyage overlong; so he ran on with the wind abeam, & his little craft leapt merrily over the sea-hills under the freshening breeze. The sun set and the moon and stars shone out, and he still sailed on, and durst not sleep, save as a dog does, with one eye. At last came dawn, and as the light grew it was a fair day with a falling wind, and a bright sky, but it clouded over before sunset, and the wind freshened from the north by east, and, would he, would he not, Hallblithe must run before it night-long, till at sunrise it fell again, and all day was too light for him to make much way beating to northward; nor did it freshen till after the moon was risen some while after sunset 🍂 And now he was so weary that he must needs sleep; so he lashed the helm, and took a reef in the sail, and ran before the wind, he sleeping in the stern.

BUT past the middle of the night, towards the dawning, he awoke with the sound of a great shout in his ears. So he looked over the dark waters, & saw nought, for the night was cloudy again. Then he trimmed his craft, and went to sleep again, for he was overburdened with slumber.

WHEN he awoke it was broad daylight; so he looked to the tiller and got the boat's head a little up to the wind, & then gazed about him with the sleep still in his eyes. And as his eyes took in the picture before him he could not refrain a cry; for lo! there arose up great & grim right ahead the black cliffs of the Isle of Ransom. Straightway he got to the sheet, & strove to wear the boat; but for all that he could do she drifted toward the land, for she was gotten into a strong current of the sea that set shoreward. So he struck sail, and took the oars and rowed mightily so that he might bear her off shore; but it availed nothing, & still he drifted landward.

SO he stood up from the oars, & turned about and looked, and saw that he was but some three furlongs from the shore, and that he was come to the very haven-mouth whence he had set sail with the Sea-eagle a twelvemonth ago: and he knew that into that haven he needs must get him, or be dashed to pieces against the high cliffs of the land: and he saw how the waves ran on to the cliffs, and whiles one higher than the others smote the rock-wall and ran up it, as if it could climb over on to the grassy lip beyond, and then fell back again, leaving a river of brine running down the steep 🍂 Then he said that he would take what might befall him inside the haven. So he hoisted sail again, & took the tiller, and steered right for the midmost of the gate between the rocks, wondering what should await him there. Then it was but a few minutes ere his bark shot into the smoothness of the haven, and presently began to lose way; for all the wind was dead within that land-locked water 🍂 Hallblithe looked steadily round about seeking his foe; but the haven was empty of ship or boat; so he ran his eye along the shore to see where he should best lay his keel and as aforesaid there was no beach there, and the water was deep right up to the grassy lip of the land; though the tides ran somewhat high, and at low water would a little steep undercliff go up from the face of the sea. But now it was near the top of the tide, and there was scarce two feet betwixt the grass and the dark-green sea.

NOW Hallblithe steered toward an ingle of the haven; & beyond it, a little way off, rose a reef of rocks out of the green grass, & thereby was a flock of sheep feeding, and a big man lying down amongst them, who seemed to be unarmed, as Hallblithe could not see any glint of steel about him.

HALLBLITHE drew nigh the shore, and the big man stirred not; nor did he any the more when the keel ran along the shore, and Hallblithe leapt out and moored his craft to his spear stuck deep in the earth. And now

Hallblithe deems that the man must be either dead or
asleep: so he drew his sword and had it in his right hand,
& in his left a sharp knife, & went straight up to the man
betwixt the sheep, and found him so lying on his side that
he could not see his face; so he stirred him with his foot, &
cried out: "Awake, O Shepherd! for dawn is long past &
day is come, and therewithal a guest for thee!" The man
turned over & slowly sat up, and, lo! who should it be but
the Puny Fox? Hallblithe started back at the sight of him,
and cried out at him, and said: "Have I found thee, O mine
enemy?"

THE Puny Fox sat up a little straighter, and rubbed his
eyes and said: "Yea, thou hast found me sure enough.
But as to my being thine enemy, a word or two may be said
about that presently" *"What!"* said Hallblithe, "dost
thou deem that aught save my sword will speak to thee?"
"I wot not," said the Puny Fox, slowly rising to his feet,
"but I suppose thou wilt not slay me unarmed, and thou
seest that I have no weapons" *"Get thee weapons, then,"*
quoth Hallblithe, "and delay not; for the sight of thee alive
sickens me" *"Ill is that,"* said the Puny Fox, "but come
thou with me at once, where I shall find both the weapons
and a good fighting-stead. Hasten! time presseth, now thou
art come at last" *"And my boat?"* said Hallblithe *"Wilt thou carry her in thy pouch?"* said the Puny Fox;
"thou wilt not need her again, whether thou slay me, or I
thee."

HALLBLITHE knit his brows on him in his wrath; for he
deemed that Fox's meaning was to threaten him with
the vengeance of the kindred. Howbeit, he said nought; for
he deemed it ill to wrangle in words with one whom he was
presently to meet in battle; so he followed as the Puny Fox
led. Fox brought him past the reef of rock aforesaid, and up
a narrow cleft of the cliffs overlooking the sea, whereby they
came into a little grass-grown meadow well nigh round in
shape, as smooth & level as a hall-floor, and fenced about by

a wall of rock: a place which had once been the mouth of an earth-fire, and a cauldron of molten stone.

WHEN they stood on the smooth grass Fox said: "Hold thee there a little, while I go to my weapon-chest, & then shall we see what is to be done." Therewith he turned aside to a cranny of the rock, and going down on his hands & knees, fell to creeping like a worm up a hole therein, which belike led to a cavern; for after his voice had come forth from the earth, grunting and groaning, and cursing this thing, and that, out he comes again feet first, and casts down an old rusty sword without a sheath; a helm no less rusty, & battered withal, and a round target, curled up and out-worn as if it would fall to pieces of itself. Then he stands up & stretches himself, & smiles pleasantly on Hallblithe and says: "Now, mine enemy, when I have donned helm and shield and got my sword in hand, we may begin the play: as to a hauberk I must needs go lack; for I could not come by it; I think the old man must have chaffered it away: he was ever too money-fain."

BUT Hallblithe looked on him angrily and said: "Hast thou brought me hither to mock me? Hast thou no better weapons wherewith to meet a warrior of the Raven than these rusty shards, which look as if thou hastrobbed a grave of the dead? I will not fight thee so armed" 🍂 "Well," said the Puny Fox, "and from out of a grave come they verily: for in that little hole lieth my father's grandsire, the great Sea-mew of the Ravagers, the father of that Sea-eagle whom thou knowest. But since thou thinkest scorn of these weapons of a dead warrior, in go the old carle's treasures again! It is as well maybe; since he might be wrath beyond his wont if he were to wake and miss them; and already this cold cup of the once-boiling rock is not wholly safe because of him."

SO he crept into the hole once more, and out of it presently, and stood smiting his palms one against the other to dust them, like a man who has been handling parchments long laid by; and Hallblithe stood looking at him, still wrathful, but silent.

THEN said the Puny Fox: "This at least was a wise word of thine, that thou wouldst not fight me. For the end of fighting is slaying; and it is stark folly to fight without slaying; and now I see that thou desirest not to slay me: for if thou didst, why didst thou refuse to fall on me armed with the ghosts of weapons that I borrowed from a ghost? Nay, why didst thou not slay me as I crept out of yonder hole? Thou wouldst have had a cheap bargain of me either way. It would be rank folly to fight me" 🖋 Said Hallblithe hoarsely: "Why didst thou bewray me, & lie to me, and lure me away from the quest of my beloved, and waste a whole year of my life?" 🖋 "It is a long story," said the Puny Fox, "which I may tell thee some day. Meantime I may tell thee this, that I was compelled thereto by one far mightier than I, to wit the Undying King."

AT that word the smouldering wrath blazed up in Hallblithe, & he drew his sword hastily and hewed at the Puny Fox: but he leapt aside nimbly and ran in on Hallblithe, and caught his sword-arm by the wrist, & tore the weapon out of his hand, and overbore him by sheer weight and stature, and drave him to the earth. Then he rose up, and let Hallblithe rise also, and took his sword and gave it into his hand again and said: "Crag-nester, thou art wrathful, but little. Now thou hast thy sword again and mayst slay me if thou wilt. Yet not until I have spoken a word to thee: so hearken! or else by the Treasure of the Sea I will slay thee with my bare hands. For I am strong indeed in this place with my old kinsman beside me. Wilt thou hearken?"

SPEAK," said Hallblithe, "I hearken." Said the Puny Fox: "True it is that I lured thee away from thy quest, and wore away a year of thy life. Yet true it is also that I repent me thereof, and ask thy pardon. What sayest thou?"

HALLBLITHE spake not, but the heat died out of his face and he was become somewhat pale. Said the Puny Fox: "Dost thou not remember, O Raven, how thou badest me battle last year on the sea-shore by the side of the Rollers of the Raven? and how this was to be the prize of battle, that the vanquished should serve the vanquisher year-long, and do all his will? And now this prize and more thou hast won without battle; for I swear by the Treasure of the Sea, and by the bones of the great Sea-mew yonder, that I will serve thee not year-long but life-long, and that I will help thee in thy quest for thy beloved. What sayest thou?"

HALLBLITHE stood speechless a moment, looking past the Puny Fox, rather than at him. Then the sword tumbled out of his hand on to the grass, & great tears rolled down his cheeks and fell on to his raiment, and he reached out his hand to the Puny Fox and said: "O friend, wilt thou not bring me to her? for the days wear, and the trees are growing old round about the Acres of the Raven."

THEN the Puny Fox took his hand; & laughed merrily in his face, and said: "Great is thine heart, O Carrion-biter! But now that thou art my friend I will tell thee that I have a deeming of the whereabouts of thy beloved. Or where deemest thou was the garden wherein thou sawest her standing on the page of the book in that dream of the night? So it is, O Raven-son, that it is not for nothing that my grandsire's father lieth in yonder hole of the rocks; for of late he hath made me wise in mighty lore. Thanks have thou, O kinsman!" And he turned him toward the rock wherein was the grave. But Hallblithe said: "What is to do now? Am I not in a land of foemen?" "Yea, forsooth," said the Puny Fox, "and even if thou knewest where thy love is, thou shouldst hardly escape from this isle unslain, save for me." Said Hallblithe: "Is there not my bark, that I might depart at once? for I deem not that the Hostage is on the Isle of Ransom."

THE Puny Fox laughed boisterously & said: "Nay, she is not. But as to thy boat, there is so strong a set of the flood-tide toward this end of the isle, that with the wind blowing as now, from the north-north-east, thou mayst not get off the shore for four hours at least, and I misdoubt me that within that time we shall have tidings of a ship of ours coming into the haven. Thy bark they shall take, and thee also if thou art therein; and then soon were the story told, for they know thee for a rebel of the Undying King. Hearken! Dost thou not hear the horn's voice? Come up hither and we shall see what is towards."

SO saying, he led hastily up a kind of stair in the rock-wall, until they reached a cranny, whence through a hole in the cliff, they could see all over the haven. And lo! as they looked, in the very gate and entry of it came a great ship heaving up her bows on the last swell of the outer sea (where the wind had risen somewhat), and rolling into the smooth, land-locked water. Black was her sail, and the image of the Sea-eagle enwrought thereon spread wide over it; and the banner of the Flaming Sword streamed out from the stern. Many men all-weaponed were on the decks, and the minstrels high up on the poop were blowing a merry song of return on their battle-horns.

LO, you," said the Puny Fox, "thy luck or mine hath served thee this time, in that the Flaming Sword did not overhaul thee ere thou madest the haven. We are well here at least" 🗡 Said Hallblithe: "But may not some of them come up hither perchance?" 🗡 "Nay, nay," said the Puny Fox; "they fear the old man in the cleft yonder; for he is not over guest-fain. This mead is mine own, as for other living men; it is my unroofed house, and I have here a house with a roof also, which I will show thee presently. For now since the Flaming Sword hath come, there is no need for haste; nay, we cannot depart till they have gone up-country. So I will show thee presently what we shall do to-night."

SO there they sat and watched those men bring their ship to the shore and moor her hard by Hallblithe's boat. They cried out when they saw her, & when they were aland they gathered about her to note her build, and the fashion of the spear whereto she was tied. Then in a while the more part of them, some four-score in number, departed up the valley toward the great house & left none but a half dozen ship-warders behind 🖋 "Seest thou, friend of the Ravens," said the Fox, "hadst thou been there, they might have done with thee what they would. Did I not well to bring thee into my unroofed house?" 🖋 "Yea, verily," said Hallblithe; "but will not some of the ship-wards, or some of the others returning, come up hither and find us? I shall yet lay my bones in this evil island" 🖋 The Puny Fox laughed, & said: "It is not so bad as thy sour looks would have it; anyhow it is good enough for a grave, and at this present I may call it a casket of precious things." "What meanest thou?" said Hallblithe eagerly 🖋 "Nay, nay," said the other, "nought but what thou knowest. Art thou not therein, and I myself? without reckoning the old carle in the hole yonder. But I promise thee thou shalt not die here this time, unless thou wilt. And as to folk coming up hither, I tell thee again they durst not; because they fear my great-grand-sire over much. Not that they are far wrong therein; for now he is dead, the worst of him seemeth to come out of him, and he is not easily dealt with, save by one who hath some share of his wisdom. Thou thyself couldst see by my kinsman, the Sea-eagle, how much of ill blood and churlish malice there may be in our kindred when they wax old, and loneliness and dreariness taketh hold of them. For I must tell thee that I have oft heard my father say that his father the Sea-eagle was in his youth and his prime blithe and buxom, a great lover of women, and a very friendly fellow. But ever, as I say, as the men of our kind wax in years, they worsen; and thereby mayst thou deem how bad the old man in yonder must be, since he hath lain so long in the grave. But now we will go to that house of mine on the other side of the mead, over against my kinsman's."

HEREWITH he led Hallblithe down from the rock while Hallblithe said to him: "What! art thou also dead that thou hast a grave here?" "Nay, nay," said Fox, smiling, "am I so evil-conditioned then? I am no older than thou art" "But tell me," said Hallblithe, "wilt thou also wax evil as thou growest old?" "Maybe not," said Fox, looking hard at him, "for in my mind it is that I may be taken into another house, and another kindred, and amongst them I shall be healed of much that might turn to ill."

HEREWITH were they come across the little meadow to a place where was a cave in the rock closed with a door, and a wicket window therein. Fox led Hallblithe into it, and within it was no ill dwelling; for it was dry and clean, & there were stools therein and a table, & shelves and lockers in the wall. When they had sat them down Fox said: "Here mightst thou dwell safely as long as thou wouldst, if thou wouldst risk dealings with the old carle. But, as I wot well that thou art in haste to be gone and get home to thy kin-dred, I must bring thee at dusk to-day close up to our feast-hall, so that thou mayst be at hand to do what hath to be done to-night, so that we may get us gone to-morrow. Also thou must do off thy Raven gear lest we meet any in the twi-light as we go up to the house; & here have I to hand home-spun raiment such as our war-taken thralls wear, which shall serve thy turn well enough; but this thou needst not do on till the time is at hand for our departure; and then I will bring thee away, and bestow thee in a bower hard by the hall; and when thou art within, I may so look to it that none shall go in there, or if they do, they shall see nought in thee save a carle known to them by name. My kinsman hath learned me to do harder things than this. But now it is time to eat and drink."

HEREWITH he drew victual from out a locker and they fell to. But when they had eaten, Fox taught Hallblithe what he should do in the hall that night, as shall be told hereafter. And then, with much talk about many things, they wore away the day in that ancient cup of the seething rock, & a little before dusk set out for the hall, bearing with them Hallblithe's gear bundled up together, as though it had been wares from over sea. So they came to the house before the tables were set, and the Puny Fox bestowed Hallblithe in a bower which gave into the buttery, so that it was easy to go straight into the mid-most of the hall. There was Hallblithe clad and armed in his Raven gear; but Fox gave him a vizard to go over his face, so that none might know him when he entered therein.

CHAPTER XXI: OF THE FIGHT OF THE CHAMPIONS IN THE HALL OF THE RAVAGERS

NOW it is to be told that the chieftains came into the hall that night and sat down at the board on the dais, even as Hallblithe had seen them do aforetime. And the chieftain of all, who was called the Erne of the Sea-eagles, rose up according to custom & said: "Hearken, folk! this is a night of the champions, whereon we may not eat till the pale blades have clashed together, and one hath vanquished & another been overcome. Now let them stand forth and give out the prize of victory which the vanquished shall pay to the vanquisher. And let it be known, that, whosoever may be the champion that winneth the battle, whether he be a kinsman, or an alien, or a foeman declared; yea, though he have left the head of my brother at the hall-door, he shall pass this night with us safe from sword, safe from axe, safe from hand: he shall eat as we eat, drink as we drink, sleep as we sleep, & depart safe from any hand or weapon, & shall sail the sea at his pleasure in his own keel or in ours, as to him and us may be meet. Blow up horns for the champions!"

SO the horns blew a cheerful strain, and when they were done, there came into the hall a tall man clad in black, and with black armour and weapons saving the white blade of his sword. He had a vizard over his face, but his hair came down from under his helm like the tail of a red horse.

SO he stood amidst the floor and cried out: "I am the champion of the Ravagers. But I swear by the Treasure of the Sea that I will cross no blade to-night save with an alien, a foeman of the kindred. Hearest thou, O chieftain, O Erne of the Sea-eagles?"

HEAR it I do," said the chieftain, "and I deem that thy meaning is that we should go supperless to bed; and this cometh of thy perversity: for we know thee despite thy vizard. Belike thou deemest that thou shalt not be met this even, and that there is no free alien in the island to draw sword against thee. But beware! For when we came aland this morning we found a skiff of the aliens tied to a great spear stuck in the bank of the haven; so that there will be one foeman at least abroad in the island. But we said that if we should come on the man, we would set his head on the gable of the hall with the mouth open toward the North for a token of reproach to the dwellers in the land over sea. But now give out the prize of victory, and I swear by the Treasure of the Sea that we will abide by thy word."

SAID the champion: "These are the terms & conditions of the battle; that whichso of us is vanquished, he shall either die, or serve the vanquisher for twelve moons, to fare with him at his will, to go his errands, & do according to his commandment in all wise. Hearest thou, chieftain?" "Yea," said he, "& by the Undying King, both thou and we shall abide by this bargain. So look to it that thou smite great strokes, lest our hall lack a gable-knop. Horns, blow up for the alien champion!" So again the horns were winded; and ere their voice had died, in from the buttery screens came a glittering image of war, and there stood the alien champion over against the warrior of the sea; and he too had a vizard over his face.

NOW when the folk saw him, & how slim and light and small he looked beside their champion, and they beheld the Raven painted on his white shield, they hooted and laughed for scorn of him and his littleness. But he tossed his sword up lightly and caught it by the hilts as it fell, and drew nigher to the champion of the sea and stood facing him within reach of his sword Then the chieftain on the high-seat put his two hands to his mouth and roared out: "Fall on, ye champions, fall on!"

BUT the folk in the hall were so eager that they stood on the benches and the boards, and craned over each other's shoulders, so that they might lose no whit of the hand-play. Now flashed the blades in the candle-lit hall, and the red-haired champion hove up his sword and smote two great strokes to right and to left; but the alien gave way before him, & the folk cried out at him in scorn and in joy of their champion, who fell to raining down great strokes like the hail amidst the lightning. But so deft was the alien, that he stood amidst it unhurt, and laid many strokes on his foeman, and did all so lightly & easily, that it seemed as if he were dancing rather than fighting; and the folk held their peace and began to doubt if their huge champion would prevail. Now the red-haired fetched a mighty stroke at the alien, who leapt aside lightly & gat his sword in his left hand & dealt a great stroke on the other's head, and the red-haired staggered, for he had over-reached himself; & again the alien smote him a left-handed stroke so that he fell full length on the floor with a mighty clatter, and the sword flew out of his hand: and the folk were dumb-founded.

WHEN the alien threw himself on the sea-champion, and knelt upon him, & shortened his sword as if to slay him with a thrust. But thereon the man overthrown cried out: "Hold thine hand, for I am vanquished! Now give me peace according to the bargain struck between us, that I shall serve thee year-long, and follow thee wheresoever thou goest."

THEREWITH the alien champion arose and stood off from him, and the man of the sea gat to his feet, and did off his helm, so that all men could see that he was the Puny Fox.

THEN the victorious champion unhelmed himself, and lo, it was Hallblithe! And a shout arose in the hall, part of wonder, part of wrath ❧ Then cried out the Puny Fox: "I call on all men here to bear witness that by reason of this battle, Hallblithe of the Ravens is free to come & go as he will in the Isle of Ransom, & to take help of any man that will help him, & to depart from the isle when he will & how he will, taking me with him if so he will" ❧ Said the chieftain: "Yea, this is right & due, and so shall it be. But now, since no freeman, who is not a foe of the passing hour, may abide in our hall without eating of our meat, come up here, Hallblithe, and sit by me, & eat and drink of the best we have, since the Norns would not give us thine head for a gable-knop. But what wilt thou do with thy thrall the Puny Fox; & whereto in the hall wilt thou have him shown? Or wilt thou that he sit fasting in the darkness to-night, laid in gyves and fetters? Or shall he have the cheer of whipping and stripes, as befitteth a thrall to whom the master oweth a grudge? What is thy will with him?" ✒ Said Hallblithe: "My will is that thou give him a seat next to me, whether that be high or low, or the bench of thy prison-house. That he eat of my dish, & drink of my cup, whatsoever the meat and drink may be. For to-morrow I mean that we twain shall go under the earth-collar together, & that our blood shall run together and that we shall be brothers in arms henceforward." Then Hallblithe did on his helm again and drew his sword, and looked aside to the Puny Fox to bid him do the like, and he did so, & Hallblithe said: "Chieftain, thou hast bidden me to table, and I thank thee; but I will not set my teeth in meat, out of our own house and land, which hath not been truly given to me by one who wotteth of me, unless I have conquered it as a prey of battle; neither will I cast a lie into the loving-cup which shall pass from thy lips to mine: therefore I will tell thee, that though I laid a stroke or two on the Puny Fox, and those no light ones, yet was this battle nought true and real, but a mere beguiling, even as that which I saw foughten in this hall aforetime, when meseemeth the slain men rose up in time to drink the good-night cup. Therefore, O men of the Ravagers, & thou, O Puny Fox, there is nought to bind your hands and refrain your hearts, & ye may slay me if ye will without murder or dis-honour, and may make the head of Hallblithe a knop for your feast-hall. Yet shall one or two fall to earth before I fall."

HEREWITH he shook his sword aloft, & a great roar arose, and weapons came down from the wall, & the candles shone on naked steel. But the Puny Fox came & stood by Hallblithe, and spake in his ear amidst the uproar: "Well now, brother-in-arms, I have been trying to learn thee the lore of lies, & surely thou art the worst scholar who was ever smitten by master. And the outcome of it is that I, who

have lied so long and well, must now pay for all, and die for
a barren truth" 🖋 Said Hallblithe: "Let all be as it will! I
love thee, lies and all; but as for me I cannot handle them.
Lo you! great and grim shall be the slaying, and we shall not
fall unavenged" 🖋 Said the Puny Fox: "Hearken! for still
they hang back. Belike it is I that have drawn this death on
thee and me. My last lie was a fool's lie and we die for it: for
what wouldst thou have done hadst thou wotted that thy
beloved, the Hostage of the Rose:" ... He broke off perforce;
for Hallblithe was looking to right & left and handling his
sword, and heard not that last word of his; and from both
sides of the hall the throng was drawing round about those
twain, weapon in hand. Then Hallblithe set his eyes on a big
man in front who was heaving up a heavy short-sword and
thought that he would at least slay this one. But or ever he
might smite, the great horn blared out over the tumult, and
men forbore a while and fell somewhat silent.

THEN came down to them the voice of the chieftain, a
loud voice, but clear and with mirth mingled with anger
in it, and he said: "What do these fools of the Ravagers cum-
bering the floor of the feast-hall, & shaking weapons when
there is no foeman anigh? Are they dreaming-drunk before
the wine is poured? Why do they not sit down in their places,
and abide the bringing in of the meat? And ye women, where
are ye, why do ye delay our meat, when ye may well wot
that our hearts are drooping for hunger; and all hath been
duly done, the battle of the champions fought and won, and
the prize of war given forth and taken? How long, O folk,
shall your chieftains sit fasting?" 🖋 Then there arose great
laughter in the hall, and men withdrew them from those
twain and went and sat them down in their places 🖋 Then
the chieftain said: "Come up hither, I say, O Hallblithe, and
bring thy war-thrall with thee if thou wilt. But delay not,
unless it be so that thou art neither hungry nor thirsty; and
good sooth thou shouldst be both; for men say that the
ravens are hard to satisfy. Come then & make good cheer
with us!" So Hallblithe thrust his sword into the sheath,

and the Puny Fox did the like, and they went both together
up the hall to the high-seat. And Hallblithe sat down on the
chieftain's right hand, and the Puny Fox next to him; and
the chieftain, the Erne, said: "O Hallblithe, dost thou need
thine armour at table; or dost thou find it handy to take thy
meat clad in thy byrny and girt with a sword?" 🍃 Then
laughed Hallblithe and said: "Nay, meseemeth to-night I
shall need war-gear no more." And he stood up and did off
all his armour & gave it, sword and all, into the hands of a
woman, who bore it off, he knew not whither. And the Erne
looked on him and said: "Well is that! and now I see that
thou art a fair young man, & it is no marvel though maidens desire thee." As he spake came in the damsels with the
victual and the cheer was exceeding good, and Hallblithe
grew light-hearted.

BUT when the healths had been drunk as aforetime, and
men had drunk a cup or two thereafter, there rose a
warrior from one of the endlong benches, a big young man,
black-haired and black-bearded, ruddy of visage, and he said
in a voice that was rough & fat: "O Erne, and ye other chieftains, we have been talking here at our table concerning this
guest of thine who hath beguiled us, and we are not wholly
at one with thee as to thy dealings with him. True it is, now
that the man hath our meat in his belly, that he must depart
from amongst us with a whole skin, unless of his own will he
stand up to fight some man of us here. Yet some of us think
that he is not so much our friend that we should help him to
a keel whereon to fare home to those that hate us: and we
say that it would not be unlawful to let the man abide in the
isle, & proclaim him a wolf's-head within a half-moon of to-
day. Or what sayest thou?" 🍃 Said the Erne: "Wait for my
word a while, and hearken to another! Is the Grey-goose of
the Ravagers in the hall? Let him give out his word on this
matter."

THEN arose a white-headed carle from a table nigh to
the dais, whose black raiment was well adorned with

gold. Despite his years his face was fair & little wrinkled; a
man with a straight nose and a well-fashioned mouth, and
with eyes still bright and grey. He spake: "O folk, I find
that the Erne hath done well in cherishing this guest. For
first, if he hath beguiled us, he did it not save by the furtherance and sleight of our own kinsman; therefore if any
one is to die for beguiling us, let it be the Puny Fox. Secondly, we may well wot that heavy need hath driven the
man to this beguilement; and I say that it was no unmanly
deed for him to enter our hall and beguile us with his
sleight; and that he hath played out the play right well and
cunningly with the wisdom of a warrior. Thirdly, the manli-
ness of him is well proven, in that having overcome us in
sleight, he hath spoken out the sooth concerning our
beguilement and hath made himself our foeman and captive, when he might have sat down by us as our guest,
freely and in all honour. And this he did, not as contemning
the Puny Fox and his lies and crafty wiles (for he hath told
us that he loveth him); but so that he might show himself a
man in that which trieth manhood. Moreover, ye shall not
forget that he is the rebel of the Undying King, who is our
lord and master; therefore in cherishing him we show ourselves great-hearted, in that we fear not the wrath of our
master. Therefore I naysay the word of the War-brand that
we should make this man a wolf's-head; for in so doing we
shall show ourselves lesser-hearted than he is, & of no
account beside of him; and his head on our hall-gable should
be to us a nithing-stake, and a tree of reproach. So I bid
thee, O Erne, to make much of this man; and thou shalt do
well to give him worthy gifts, such as warriors may take, so
that he may show them at home in the House of the Raven,
that it may be the beginning of peace betwixt us and his
noble kindred. This is my say, and later on I shall wax no
wiser."

HEREWITH he sat down, and there arose a murmur
and stir in the hall; but the more part said that the

Grey-goose had spoken well, and that it was good to be at peace with such manly fellows as the new guest was *✦* But the Erne said: "One word will I lay hereto, to wit, that he who desireth mine enmity let him do scathe to Hall-blithe of the Ravens and hinder him." Then he bade fill round the cups, and called a health to Hallblithe, and all men drank to him, and there was much joyance and merriment.

BUT when the night was well worn, the Erne turned to Hallblithe and said: "That was a good word of the Grey-goose which he spake concerning the giving of gifts: Raven-son, wilt thou take a gift of me and be my friend?" *✦* "Thy friend will I be," said Hallblithe, "but no gift will I take of thee or any other till I have the gift of gifts, and that is my troth-plight maiden. I will not be glad, till I can be glad with her." Then laughed the Erne, and the Puny Fox grinned all across his wide face, and Hallblithe looked from one to the other of them and wondered at their mirth, and when they saw his wondering eyes, they did but laugh the more; and the Erne said: "Nevertheless, thou shalt see the gift which I would give thee; and then mayst thou take it or leave it as thou wilt. Ho ye! bring in the throne of the Eastlands with them that minister to it!" Certain men left the hall as he spake, and came back bearing with them a throne fashioned most goodly of ivory, parcel-gilt & begemmed, and adorned with marvellous craftsmanship: and they set it down amidst of the hall-floor and went aback to their places, while the Erne sat & smiled kindly on the folk and on Hallblithe *✦* Then arose the sound of fiddles and the lesser harp, and the doors of the screen were opened, and there flowed into the hall a company of fair damsels not less than a score, each one with a rose on her bosom, and they came & stood in order behind the throne of the Eastlands, and they strewed roses on the ground before them: and when they were duly ranged they fell to singing:

OW waneth spring,
While all birds sing,
And the south wind blows
The earliest rose
To and fro
By the doors we know,
And the scented gale
Fills every dale.

Slow now are brooks running
because of the weed,
And the thrush hath no cunning
to hide her at need,
So swift as she flieth
from hedge-row to tree,
As one that toil trieth,
and deedful must be.

ND O! that at last,
All sorrows past,
This night I lay
'Neath the oak-beams grey!
O, to wake from sleep
To see dawn creep
Through the fruitful grove
Of the house that I love!

O! my feet to be treading
the threshold once more,
O'er which once went the leading
of swords to the war!
O! my feet in the garden's
edge under the sun,
Where the seeding grass hardens
for haysel begun!

O, lo! the wind blows
To the heart of the Rose,

And the ship lies tied
To the haven side!
But O for the keel
The sails to feel!
And the alien ness
Growing less and less;
As down the wind driveth
and thrusts through the sea
The sail-burg that striveth
to turn and go free,
But the lads at the tiller
they hold her in hand,
And the wind our well-willer
drives fierce to the land.

E shall wend it yet,
The highway wet;
For what is this
That our bosoms kiss?
What lieth sweet
Before our feet?
What token hath come
To lead us home?
'Tis the Rose of the garden
walled round from the croft
Where the grey roof its warden
steep riseth aloft,
'Tis the Rose 'neath the oaken-
beamed hall, where they bide,
The pledges unbroken,
the hand of the bride.

HALLBLITHE heard the song, and half thought it prom-
ised him somewhat; but then he had been so misled and
mocked at, that he scarce knew how to rejoice at it. Now the
Erne spake: "Wilt thou not take the chair & these dainty
song-birds that stand about it? Much wealth might come into
thine hall if thou wert to carry them over sea to rich men

who have no kindred, nor affinity wherein to wed, but who love women as well as other men." Said Hallblithe: "I have wealth enow were I once home again. As to these maidens, I know by the fashion of them that they are no women of the Rose, as by their song they should be. Yet will I take any of these maidens that have will to go with me & be made sisters of my sisters, & wed with the warriors of the Rose; or if they are of a kindred, & long to sit each in the house of her folk, then will we send them home over the sea with warriors to guard them from all trouble. For this gift I thank thee. As to thy throne, I bid thee keep it till a keel cometh thy way from our land, bringing fair gifts for thee & thine. For we are not so unwealthy."

THEY that sat nearby heard his words and praised them; but the Erne said: "All this is free to thee, & thou mayst do what thou wilt with the gifts given to thee. Yet shalt thou have the throne; and I have thought of a way to make thee take it. Or what sayst thou, Puny Fox?" Said the Puny Fox: "Yea if thou wilt, thou mayst, but I thought it not of thee that thou wouldst. Now is all well" Again Hallblithe looked from one to the other and wondered what they meant. But the Erne cried out: "Bring in now the sitter, who shall fill the empty throne!"

THEN again the screen-doors opened, & there came in two weaponed men, leading between them a woman clad in gold and garlanded with roses. So fair was the fashion of her face & all her body, that her coming seemed to make a change in the hall, as though the sun had shone into it suddenly. She trod the hall-floor with firm feet, and sat down on the ivory chair. But even before she was seated therein Hallblithe knew that the Hostage was under that roof and coming toward him. And the heart rose in his breast and fluttered therein, so sore he yearned toward the Daughter of the Rose, and his very speech-friend. Then he heard the Erne saying, "How now, Raven-son, wilt thou have the throne and the sitter therein, or wilt thou gainsay me once more?"

THEREAFTER he himself spake, and the sound of his voice was strange to him and as if he knew it not: "Chieftain, I will not gainsay thee, but will take thy gift, & thy friendship therewith, whatsoever hath betided. Yet would I say a word or two unto the woman that sitteth yonder. For I have been straying amongst wiles & images, & mayhappen I shall yet find this to be but a dream of the night, or a beguilement of the day." Therewith he arose from the table, & walked slowly down the hall; but it was a near thing that he did not fall a weeping before all those aliens, so full his heart was.

HE came and stood before the Hostage, & their eyes were upon each other, and for a little while they had no words. Then Hallblithe began, wondering at his voice as he spake: "Art thou a woman and my speech-friend? For many images have mocked me, & I have been encompassed by lies, and led astray by behests that have not been fulfilled. And the world hath become strange to me, and empty of friends." Then she said: "Art thou verily Hallblithe? For I also have been encompassed by lies, and beset by images of things unhelpful" "Yea," said he, "I am Hallblithe of the Ravens, wearied with desire for my troth-plight maiden." Then came the rosy colour into the fairness of her face, as the rising sun lighteth the garden of flowers in the June morning; & she said: "If thou art Hallblithe, tell me what befell to the finger-gold-ring that my mother gave me when we were both but little."

THEN his face grew happy, & he smiled, and he said: "I put it for thee one autumntide in the snake's hole in the bank above the river, amidst the roots of the old thorn-tree, that the snake might brood it, and make the gold grow greater; but when winter was over and we came to look for it, lo! there was neither ring nor snake, nor thorn-tree: for the flood had washed it all away" 🍃 Thereat she smiled most sweetly, & whereas she had been looking on him hitherto with strained and anxious eyes, she now beheld him simply and friendly; & she said: "O Hallblithe, I am a woman indeed, and thy speech-friend. This is the flesh that desireth thee, and the life that is thine, and the heart which thou rejoicest. But now tell me, who are these huge images around us, amongst whom I have sat thus, once in every moon this year past, & afterwards I was taken back to the women's bower? Are they men or mountain-giants? Will they slay us, or shut us up from the light and air? Or hast thou made peace with them? Wilt thou then dwell with me here, or shall we go back again to Cleveland by the Sea? And when, oh when, shall we depart?" He smiled and said: "Quick come thy questions, beloved. These are the folks of the Ravagers & the Sea-eagles: they be men, though fierce and wild they be. Our foes they have been, and have sundered us; but now are they our friends, and have brought us together. And to-morrow, O friend, shall we depart across the waters to Cleveland by the Sea" 🍃 She leaned forward, and was about to speak softly to him, but suddenly started back, and said: "There is a big, red-haired man, as big as any here, behind thy shoulder. Is he also a friend? What would he with us?" 🍃 So Hallblithe turned about, and beheld the Puny Fox beside him, who took up the word and spoke, smiling as a man in great glee: "O maiden of the Rose, I am Hallblithe's thrall, and his scholar, to unlearn the craft of lying, whereby I have done amiss towards both him and thee. Whereof I will tell thee all the tale soon. But now I will say that it is true that we depart to-morrow for Cleveland by the Sea, thou and he, and I in company. Now I would ask thee, Hallblithe, if thou wouldst have me bestow this gift of thine in safe-keeping to-night, since there is an end of her sitting in the hall like a graven image: and to-morrow the way will be long and wearisome, What sayest thou?" 🍃 Said the Hostage: "Shall I trust this man & go with him?" 🍃 "Yea, thou shalt trust him," said Hallblithe, "for he is trusty. And even were he not, it is meet for us of the Raven and the Rose to do as our worth biddeth us, & not to fear this folk. And it behoveth us to do after their customs since we are in their house" 🖋 "That is sooth," she said; "big man, lead me out of the hall to my place. Farewell, Hallblithe, for a little while, and then shall there be no more sundering for us."

HEREWITH she departed with the Puny Fox, and Hallblithe went back to the high-seat and sat down by the Erne, who laughed on him and said: "Thou hast taken my gift, and that is well: yet shall I tell thee that I would not have given it to thee if I could have kept it for myself in such plight as thou wilt have it. But all I could do, and the Puny Fox to help withal, availed me nought. So good luck go with thine hands. Now will we to bed, and to-morrow I will lead thee out on thy way; for to say sooth, there be some here who are not well pleased with either thee or me; and thou knowest that words are wasted on wilful men, but that deeds may avail somewhat." Therewith he cried out for the cup of goodnight, and when it was drunken, Hallblithe was shown to a fair shut-bed; even that wherein he had lain aforetime; and there he went to sleep in joy, and in good liking with all men.

CHAPTER XXII: THEY GO FROM THE ISLE OF RANSOM AND COME TO CLEVELAND BY THE SEA

IN the morning early Hallblithe arose from his bed, and when he came into the mid-hall, there was the Puny Fox and the Hostage with him; Hallblithe kissed her and embraced her, and she him; yet not like lovers long sundered, but as a man and maid betrothed are wont to do, for there were folk coming and going about the hall. Then spake the Puny Fox: "The Erne is abiding us out in the meadow yonder; for now nought will serve him but he must needs go under the earth-collar with us. How sayest thou, is he enough thy friend?" Said Hallblithe, smiling on the Hostage: "What hast thou to say to it, beloved?" "Nought at all," she said, "if thou art friend to any of these men. I may deem that I have somewhat against the chieftain, whereof belike this big man may tell thee hereafter; but even so much meseemeth I have against this man himself, who is now become thy friend and scholar; for he also strove for my beguilement, and that not for himself, but for another" 🖋 "True it is," said the Fox, "that I did it for another; even as yesterday I took thy mate Hallblithe out of the trap where-into he had strayed, and compassed his deliverance by means of the unfaithful battle; and even as I would have stolen thee for him, O Rose-maiden, if need had been; yea, even if I must have smitten into ruin the roof-tree of the Ravagers. And how could I tell that the Erne would give thee up unstolen? Yea, thou sayeth sooth, O noble and spotless maiden; all my deeds, both good and ill, have I done for others; and so I deem it shall be while my life lasteth" 🖋 Then Hallblithe laughed & said: "Art thou nettled, fellow-in-arms, at the word of a woman who knoweth thee not? She shall yet be thy friend, O Fox. But tell me, beloved, I deemed that thou hadst not seen Fox before; how then can he have helped the Erne against thee?" 🖋 "Yet she sayeth sooth," said Fox, "this was of my sleight: for when I had to come before her, I changed my skin, as I well know how; there are others in this land who can do so much as that. But what sayest thou concern-ing the brotherhood with the Erne?" 🖋 "Let it be so," said Hallblithe, "he is manly and true, though masterful, & is meet for this land of his. I shall not fall out with him; for seldom meseemeth shall I see the Isle of Ransom" 🖋 "And I never again," said the Puny Fox 🖋 "Dost thou loathe it, then," said the Hostage, "because of the evil thou hast done therein?" 🖋 "Nay," said he, "what is the evil, when henceforth I shall do but good? Nay, I love the land. Belike thou deemest it but dreary with its black rocks and black sand, and treeless wind-swept dales; but I know it in summer and winter, and sun and shade, in storm and calm. And I know where the fathers dwelt and the sons of their sons' sons have long lain in the earth. I have sailed its windiest firths, and climbed its steepest crags; and ye may well wot that it hath a friendly face to me; and the land-wights of the mountains will be sorry for my departure."

SO he spake, & Hallblithe would have answered him, but by now were they come to a grassy hollow amidst the dale, where the Erne had already made the earth-yoke ready. To wit, he had loosened a strip of turf all save the two ends, & had propped it up with two ancient dwarf-wrought spears, so that amidmost there was a lintel to go under. So when he saw those others coming, he gave them the sele of the day, and said to Hallblithe: "What is it to be? shall I be less than thy brother-in-arms henceforward?" Said Hallblithe: "Not a whit less. It is good to have brothers in other lands than one" ✒ So they made no delay, but clad in all their war-gear, they went under the earth-yoke one after the other; thereafter they stood together, and each let blood in his arm, so that the blood of all three mingled together fell down on the grass of the ancient earth; and they swore friendship and brotherhood each to each ✒ But when all was done the Erne spake: "Brother Hallblithe, as I lay awake in bed this morning I deemed that I would take ship with thee to Cleveland by the Sea, that I might dwell there a while. But when I came out of the hall, and saw the dale lying green betwixt hill-side and hill-side, and the glittering river running down amidmost, & the sheep and kine and horses feeding up and down on either side the water: and I looked up at the fells and saw how deep blue they stood up against the snowy peaks, and I thought of all our deeds on the deep sea, and the merry nights, in yonder abode of men: then I thought that I would not leave the kindred, were it but for a while, unless war and lifting called me. So now I will ride with thee to the ship, &

then farewell to thee" 🍃 "It is good," said Hallblithe, "though not as good as it might be. Glad had we been with thee in the hall of the Ravens" 🍃 As he spoke drew anigh the carles leading the horses, and with them came six of those damsels whom the Erne had given to Hallblithe the night before; two of whom asked to be brought to their kindred over sea; but the other four were fain to go with Hallblithe & the Hostage, and become their sisters at Cleveland by the Sea.

SO then they got to horse and rode down the dale toward the haven, & the carles rode with them, so that of weaponed men they were a score in company. But when they were half-way to the haven they saw where hard by three knolls on the way-side were men standing with their weapons and war-gear glittering in the sun. So the Erne laughed and said: "Shall we have a word with War-brand then?" But they rode steadily on their way, & when they came up to the knolls they saw that it was War-brand indeed with a score of men at his back; but they stirred not when they saw Erne's company that it was great. Then Erne laughed aloud and cried out in a big voice: "What, lads! ye ride early this morning; are there foemen abroad in the Isle?" 🍃 They shrank back before him, but a carle of those who was hindermost cried out: "Art thou coming back to us, Erne, or have thy new friends bought thee to lead them in battle?" 🍃 "Fear it nought," quoth Erne, "I shall be back before the shepherd's noon."

SO they went their ways and came to the haven, and there lay the Flaming Sword, and beside her a trim bark, not right great, all ready for sea: and Hallblithe's skiff was made fast to her for an after-boat. 🍃 Then the Hostage & Hallblithe and the six damsels went aboard her, and when the Erne had bidden them farewell, they cast off the hawsers and thrust her out through the haven-mouth; but ere they had got midmost of the haven, they saw the Erne, that he had turned about, and was riding up the dale with his house-carles, and each man's weapon was shining in his hand: &

they wondered if he were riding to battle with War-brand; and Fox said: "Meseemeth our brother-in-arms hath in his mind to give those waylayers an evil minute, and verily he is the man to do the same."

SO they gat them out of the haven, and the ebb-tide drave out seaward strongly, & the wind was fair for Cleveland by the Sea; and they ran speedily past the black cliffs of the Isle of Ransom, & soon were they hull down behind them. But on the afternoon of the next day they hove up the land of the kindreds, and by sunset they beached their ship on the sand by the Rollers of the Raven, and went ashore without more ado. And the strand was empty of all men, even as on the day when Hallblithe first met the Puny Fox. So then in the cool of the evening they went up toward the House of the Raven. Those damsels went together hand in hand two by two, and Hallblithe held the Hostage by the hand; but the Puny Fox went along beside them, gleeful and of many words; telling them tales of his wiles and his craft, & his skin-changing. "But now," quoth he, "I have left all that behind me in the Isle of Ransom, and have but one shape, & I would for your behoof that it were a goodlier one: and but one wisdom have I, even that which dwelleth in mine own head-bone. Yet it may be that this may avail you one time or other. But lo you! though I am thy thrall, have I not the look of a thrall-huckster from over sea leading up my wares to the cheaping-stead?" They laughed at his words and were merry, and much love there was amongst them as they went up to the House of the Raven.

BUT when they came thither they went into the garth, & there was no man therein, for it was now dusk, and the windows of the long hall were yellow with candle-light. Then said Fox: "Abide ye here a little; for I would go into the hall alone & see the conditions of thy people, O Hallblithe" "Go thou, then," said Hallblithe, "but be not rash. I counsel thee; for our folk are not over-patient when they deem they have a foe before them" The Puny Fox laughed, and said:

"So it is then the world over, that happy men are wilful and masterful." Then he drew his sword and smote on the door with the pommel, and the door opened to him and in he went: and he found that fair hall full of folk and bright with candles; and he stood amidst the floor; all men looked on him, and many knew him at once to be a man of the Ravagers, and silence fell upon the hall, but no man stirred hand against him. Then he said: "Will ye hearken to the word of an evil man, a robber of the folks?" 🍂 Spake the chieftain from the dais: "Words will not hurt us, sea-warrior; & thou art but one among many; wherefore thy might this eve is but as the might of a new-born baby. Speak, & afterwards eat and drink, and depart safe from amongst us!"

SPAKE the Puny Fox: "What is gone with Hallblithe, a fair young man of your kindred, and with the Hostage of the Rose, his troth-plight maiden?" 🍂 Then was the hush yet greater in the hall, so that you might have heard a pin drop; & the chieftain said: "It is a grief of ours that they are gone, and that none hath brought us back their dead bodies that we might lay them in the Acre of the Fathers" 🍂 Then leapt up a man from the end-long table nigh to Fox, and cried out: "Yea, folk! they are gone, and we deem that runagates of thy kindred, O new-come man, have stolen them from us; wherefor they shall one day pay us" 🍂 Then laughed the Puny Fox and said: "Some would say that stealing Hallblithe was like stealing a lion, and that he might take care of himself; though he was not as big as I am" 🍂 Said the last speaker: "Did thy kin or didst thou steal him, O evil man?" 🍂 "Yea, I stole him," quoth Fox, "but by sleight, and not by might."

THEN uprose great uproar in the hall, but the chieftain on the high-seat cried out: "Peace, peace!" and the noise abated, & the chieftain said: "Dost thou mean that thou comest hither to give us thine head for making away with Hallblithe & the Hostage?" 🍂 "I mean to ask rather," said the Fox, "what thou wilt give me for the bodies of these twain?" 🖋 Said the chieftain: "A boat-load of gold were not too much if thou shouldst live a little longer" 🍂 Quoth the Puny Fox: "Well, in anywise I will go and bring in the bodies aforesaid, and leave my reward to the goodwill of the Ravens."

HEREWITH he turned about to go, but lo! there already in the door stood Hallblithe holding the Hostage by the hand; & many in the hall saw them, for the door was wide. Then they came in and stood by the side of the Puny Fox, and all men in the hall arose & shouted for joy. But when the tumult was a little abated, the Puny Fox cried out: "O chieftain, & all ye folk! if a boat-load of gold were not too much reward for the bringing back the dead bodies of your friends, what reward shall he have who hath brought back their bodies & the souls therein?" Said the chieftain: "The man shall choose his own reward" 🍂 And the men in the hall shouted their yeasay.

THEN said the Puny Fox: "Well, then, this I choose, that ye make me one of your kindred before the fathers of old time" 🖋 They all cried out that he had chosen wisely & manfully; but Hallblithe said: "I bid you do for him no less than this; & ye shall wot that he is already my sworn brother-in-arms" 🍂 Now the chieftain cried out: "O Wanderers from over the sea, come up hither and sit with us and be merry at last!"

SO they went up to the dais, Hallblithe and the Hostage, & the Puny Fox & the six maidens withal. And since the night was yet young, the supper of the men of the Ravens was turned into the wedding-feast of Hallblithe and the Hostage, and that very night she became a wife of the Ravens, that she might bear to the House the best of men & the fairest of women.

BUT on the morrow they brought the Puny Fox to the mote-stead of the kindreds that he might stand before the fathers & be made a son of the kindred; & this they did because of the word of Hallblithe, and because they believed in the tale which he told them of the Glittering Plain and the Acre of the Undying. The four maidens also were made sisters of the House; and the other twain were sent home to their own kindred in all honour.

OF the Puny Fox it is said that he soon lost and forgot all the lore which he had learned of the ancient men, living and dead; and became as other men and was no wizard. Yet he was exceeding valiant & doughty; and he ceased not to go with Hallblithe wheresoever he went; and many deeds they did together, whereof the memory of men hath failed: but neither they nor any man of the Ravens came any more to the Glittering Plain, or heard any tidings of the folk that dwell there.

HERE ends the tale of the Glittering Plain, written by William Morris, & ornamented with 23 pictures by Walter Crane. Printed at the Kelmscott Press, Upper Mall, Hammersmith, in the Country of Middlesex, & finished on the 13th day of January, 1894.

THE ART AND CRAFT OF PRINTING, BY WILLIAM MORRIS.

A NOTE BY WILLIAM MORRIS ON HIS AIMS IN FOUNDING THE KELMSCOTT PRESS, TOGETHER WITH A SHORT DESCRIPTION OF THE PRESS BY S. C. COCKERELL.

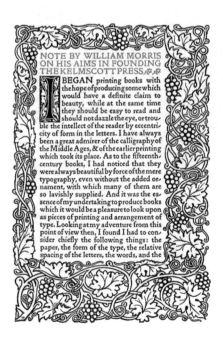

PSYCHE BORNE OFF BY ZE
PHYRUS, DRAWN BY EDWARD
BURNE·JONES & ENGRAVED
BY WILLIAM MORRIS

NOTE BY WILLIAM MORRIS ON HIS AIMS IN FOUNDING THE KELMSCOTT PRESS

began printing books with the hope of producing some which would have a definite claim to beauty, while at the same time they should be easy to read and should not dazzle the eye, or trouble the intellect of the reader by eccentricity of form in the letters. I have always been a great admirer of the calligraphy of the Middle Ages, & of the earlier printing which took its place. As to the fifteenth-century books, I had noticed that they were always beautiful by force of the mere typography, even without the added ornament, with which many of them are so lavishly supplied. And it was the essence of my undertaking to produce books which it would be a pleasure to look upon as pieces of printing and arrangement of type.

LOOKING at my adventure from this point of view then, I found I had to consider chiefly the following things: the paper, the form of the type, the relative spacing of the letters, the words, and the lines; and lastly the position of the printed matter on the page. It was a matter of course that I should consider it necessary that the paper should be hand-made, both for the sake of durability and appearance. It would be

a very false economy to stint in the quality of the paper as
to price: so I had only to think about the kind of hand-made
paper. On this head I came to two conclusions: 1st, that the
paper must be wholly of linen (most hand-made papers are of
cotton today), and must be quite 'hard,' i. e., thoroughly well
sized; and 2nd, that, though it must be 'laid' and not 'wove' (i.
e., made on a mould made of obvious wires), the lines caused
by the wires of the mould must not be too strong, so as to
give a ribbed appearance. I found that on these points I was
at one with the practice of the paper-makers of the fifteenth
century; so I took as my model a Bolognese paper of about
1473. My friend Mr. Batchelor, of Little Chart, Kent, carried
out my views very satisfactorily, and produced from the first
the excellent paper, which I still use.

NEXT as to type. By instinct rather than by conscious thinking it over, I began by getting myself a fount of Roman type.
And here what I wanted was letter pure in form; severe,
without needless excrescences; solid, without the thickening
and thinning of the line, which is the essential fault of the
ordinary modern type, and which makes it difficult to read;
and not compressed laterally, as all later type has grown
to be owing to commercial exigencies. There was only one
source from which to take examples of this perfected Roman
type, to wit, the works of the great Venetian printers of the
fifteenth century, of whom Nicholas Jenson produced the
completest and most Roman characters from 1470 to 1476.
This type I studied with much care, getting it photographed
to a big scale, and drawing it over many times before I began
designing my own letter; so that though I think I mastered
the essence of it, I did not copy it servilely; in fact, my Roman
type, especially in the lower case, tends rather more to the
Gothic than does Jenson's.

AFTER a while I felt that I must have a Gothic as well as a
Roman fount; and herein the task I set myself was to redeem
the Gothic character from the charge of unreadableness
which is commonly brought against it. And I felt that this

charge could not be reasonably brought against the types of the first two decades of printing: that Schoeffer at Mainz, Mentelin at Strasburg, and Gunther Zainer at Augsburg, avoided the spiky ends and undue compression which lay some of the later type open to the above charge. Only the earlier printers (naturally following therein the practice of their predecessors the scribes) were very liberal of contractions, and used an excess of 'tied' letters, which, by the way, are very useful to the compositor. So I entirely eschewed contractions, except for the '&,' and had very few tied letters, in fact none but the absolutely necessary ones.

KEEPING my end steadily in view, I designed a black-letter type which I think I may claim to be as readable as a Roman one, and to say the truth I prefer it to the Roman. This type is of the size called Great Primer (the Roman type is of 'English' size); but later on I was driven by the necessities of the Chaucer (a double-columned book) to get a smaller Gothic type of Pica size.

THE punches for all these types, I may mention, were cut for me with great intelligence and skill by Mr. E. P. Prince, and render my designs most satisfactorily.

NOW as to the spacing: First, the 'face' of the letter should be as nearly conterminous with the 'body' as possible, so as to avoid undue whites between the letters. Next, the lateral spaces between the words should be (a) no more than is necessary to distinguish clearly the division into words, and (b) should be as nearly equal as possible. Modern printers, even the best, pay very little heed to these two essentials of seemly composition, and the inferior ones run riot in licentious spacing, thereby producing, inter alia, those ugly rivers of lines running about the page which are such a blemish to decent printing. Third, the whites between the lines should not be excessive; the modern practice of 'leading' should be used as little as possible, and never without some definite reason, such as marking some special piece of printing. The only leading I have allowed myself is in some cases a 'thin' lead between the lines of my Gothic pica type: in the Chaucer and the double-columned books I have used a 'hair' lead, and not even this in the 16mo books.

Lastly, but by no means least, comes the position of the printed matter on the page. This should always leave the inner margin the narrowest, the top somewhat wider, the outside (fore-edge) wider still, and the bottom widest of all. This rule is never departed from in mediæval books, written or printed. Modern printers systematically transgress against it; thus apparently contradicting the fact that the unit of a book is not one page, but a pair of pages. A friend, the librarian of one of our most important private libraries, tells me that after careful testing he has come to the conclusion that the mediæval rule was to make a difference of 20 per cent. from margin to margin. Now these matters of spacing and position are of the greatest importance in the production of beautiful books; if they are properly considered they will make a book printed in quite ordinary type at least decent and pleasant to the eye. The disregard of them will spoil the effect of the best designed type.

IT was only natural that I, a decorator by profession, should attempt to ornament my books suitably: about this matter, I will only say that I have always tried to keep in mind the necessity for making my decoration a part of the page of type. I may add that in designing the magnificent and inimitable woodcuts which have adorned several of my books, and will above all adorn the Chaucer which is now drawing near completion, my friend Sir Edward Burne-Jones has never lost sight of this important point, so that his work will not only give us a series of most beautiful and imaginative pictures, but form the most harmonious decoration possible to the printed book.

KELMSCOTT HOUSE, UPPER MALL, HAMMERSMITH. NOV. 11, 1895

A SHORT HISTORY AND DESCRIPTION OF THE KELMSCOTT PRESS.

THE FOREGOING ARTICLE WAS WRITTEN AT THE REQUEST OF A
LONDON BOOKSELLER FOR AN AMERICAN CLIENT WHO WAS ABOUT
TO READ A PAPER ON THE KELMSCOTT PRESS. AS THE PRESS IS
NOW CLOSING, AND ITS SEVEN YEARS' EXISTENCE WILL SOON BE A
MATTER OF HISTORY, IT SEEMS FITTING TO SET DOWN SOME OTHER
FACTS CONCERNING IT WHILE THEY CAN STILL BE VERIFIED; THE
MORE SO AS STATEMENTS FOUNDED ON IMPERFECT INFORMA-
TION HAVE APPEARED FROM TIME TO TIME IN NEWSPAPERS AND
REVIEWS.

S early as 1866 an edition of The Earthly
Paradise was projected, which was to have
been a folio in double columns, profusely
illustrated by Sir Edward Burne-Jones, and
typographically superior to the books of that
time. The designs for the stories of Cupid
and Psyche, Pygmalion and the Image, The Ring given to
Venus, and the Hill of Venus, were finished, and forty-four
of those for Cupid and Psyche were engraved on wood in
line, somewhat in the manner of the early German masters.
About thirty-five of the blocks were executed by William
Morris himself, and the remainder by George Y. Wardle,
G. F. Campfield, C. J. Faulkner, and Miss Elizabeth Bur-
den. Specimen pages were set up in Caslon type, and in the
Chiswick Press type afterwards used in The House of the
Wolfings, but for various reasons the project went no further.
Four or five years later there was a plan for an illustrated

edition of Love is Enough, for which two initial L's and seven side ornaments were drawn and engraved by William Morris. Another marginal ornament was engraved by him from a design by Sir E. Burne-Jones, who also drew a picture for the frontispiece, which has now been engraved by W. H. Hooper for the final page of the Kelmscott Press edition of the work. These side ornaments. . . are more delicate than any that were designed for the Kelmscott Press, but they show that when the Press was started the idea of reviving some of the decorative features of the earliest printed books had been long in its founder's mind. At this same period, in the early seventies, he was much absorbed in the study of ancient manuscripts, and in writing out and illuminating various books, including a Horace and an Omar Khayyám, which may have led his thoughts away from printing. In any case, the plan of an illustrated Love is Enough, like that of the folio Earthly Paradise, was abandoned.

ALTHOUGH the books written by William Morris continued to be reasonably printed, it was not until about 1888 that he again paid much attention to typography. He was then, and for the rest of his life, when not away from Hammersmith, in daily communication with his friend and neighbour Emery Walker, whose views on the subject coincided with his own, and who had besides a practical knowledge of the technique of printing. These views were first expressed in an article by Mr. Walker in the catalogue of the exhibition of the Arts and Crafts Exhibition Society, held at the New Gallery in the autumn of 1888.

AS a result of many conversations, The House of the Wolfings was printed at the Chiswick Press at this time, with a special type modelled on an old Basel fount, unleaded, and with due regard to proportion in the margins. The title-page was also carefully arranged. In the following year The Roots of the Mountains was printed with the same type (except the lower case e), but with a differently proportioned page, and with shoulder-notes instead of head-lines. This book was published in November, 1889, and its author declared it to be the best-looking book issued since the seventeenth century. Instead of large paper copies, which had been found unsatisfactory in the case of The House of the Wolfings, two hundred and fifty copies were printed on Whatman paper of about the same size as the paper of the ordinary copies. A small stock of this paper remained over, and in order to dispose of it seventy-five copies of the translation of the Gunnlaug Saga, which first appeared in the Fortnightly Review of January, 1869, and afterwards in Three Northern Love Stories, were printed at the Chiswick Press. The type used was a black-letter copied from one of Caxton's founts, and the initials were left blank to be rubricated by hand. Three copies were printed on vellum. This little book was not however finished until November, 1890.

MEANWHILE William Morris had resolved to design a type of his own. Immediately after The Roots of the Mountains appeared, he set to work upon it, and in December, 1889, he asked Mr. Walker to go into partnership with him as a printer. This offer was declined by Mr. Walker; but, though not concerned with the financial side of the enterprise, he was virtually a partner in the Kelmscott Press from its first beginnings to its end, and no important step was taken without his advice and approval. Indeed, the original intention was to have the books set up in Hammersmith and printed at his office in Clifford's Inn.

IT was at this time that William Morris began to collect the mediæval books of which he formed so fine a library in the next six years. He had made a small collection of such books years before, but had parted with most of them, to his great regret. He now bought with the definite purpose of studying the type and methods of the early printers. Among the first books so acquired was a copy of Leonard of Arezzo's History of Florence, printed at Venice by Jacobus Rubeus in 1476, in a Roman type very similar to that of Nicholas Jenson. Parts of this book and of Jenson's Pliny of 1476 were enlarged by

photography in order to bring out more clearly the charac-
teristics of the various letters; and having mastered both
their virtues and defects, William Morris proceeded to design
the fount of type which, in the list of December, 1892, he
named the Golden type, from The Golden Legend, which
was to have been the first book printed with it. This fount
consists of eighty-one designs, including stops, figures, and
tied letters. The lower case alphabet was finished in a few
months. The first letter having been cut in Great Primer size
by Mr. Prince, was thought too large, and 'English' was the
size resolved upon. By the middle of August, 1890, eleven
punches had been cut. At the end of the year the fount was
all but complete.

ON Jan. 12th, 1891, a cottage, No. 16, Upper Mall, was
taken. Mr. William Bowden, a retired master-printer, had
already been engaged to act as compositor and pressman.
Enough type was then cast for a trial page, which was set
up and printed on Saturday, Jan. 31st, on a sample of the
paper that was being made for the Press by J. Batchelor and
Son. About a fortnight later ten reams of paper were delivered. On Feb. 18th a good supply of type followed. Mr. W. H.
Bowden, who subsequently became overseer, then joined his
father as compositor, and the first chapters of The Glittering
Plain were set up.

THE first sheet appears to have been printed on March
2nd, when the staff was increased to three by the addition
of a pressman named Giles, who left as soon as the book
was finished. A friend who saw William Morris on the day
after the printing of the page above mentioned recalls his
elation at the success of his new type. The first volume of
the Saga Library, a creditable piece of printing, was brought
out and put beside this trial page, which much more than
held its own. The poet then declared his intention to set to
work immediately on a black-letter fount; illness, however,
intervened and it was not begun until June. The lower case
alphabet was finished by the beginning of August, with the

exception of the tied letters, the designs for which, with those for the capitals, were sent to Mr. Prince on September 11th. Early in November enough type was cast for two trial pages, the one consisting of twenty-six lines of Chaucer's Franklin's Tale and the other of sixteen lines of Sigurd the Volsung. In each of these a capital I is used that was immediately discarded. On the last day of 1891 the full stock of Troy type was despatched from the foundry. Its first appearance was in a paragraph, announcing the book from which it took its name, in the list dated May, 1892.

THIS Troy type, which its designer preferred to either of the others, shows the influence of the beautiful early types of Peter Schoeffer of Mainz, Gunther Zainer of Augsburg, and Anthony Koburger of Nuremberg; but, even more than the Golden type, it has a strong character of its own, which differs largely from that of any mediæval fount. It has recently been pirated abroad, and is advertised by an enterprising German firm as 'Die amerikanische Triumph-Gothisch.' The Golden type has perhaps fared worse in being remodelled in the United States, whence, with much of its character lost, it has found its way back to England under the names 'Venetian,' 'Italian,' and 'Jenson.' It is strange that no one has yet had the good sense to have the actual type of Nicholas Jenson reproduced.

THE third type used at the Kelmscott Press, called the 'Chaucer,' differs from the Troy type only in size, being Pica instead of Great Primer. It was cut by Mr. Prince between February and May, 1892, and was ready in June. Its first appearance is in the list of chapters and glossary of The Recuyell of the Historyes of Troye, which was issued on November 24th, 1892.

ON June 2nd of that year, William Morris wrote to Mr. Prince: 'I believe in about three months' time I shall be ready with a new set of sketches for a fount of type on English body.' These sketches were not forthcoming; but on Nov.

5th, 1892, he bought a copy of Augustinus De Civitate Dei, printed at the Monastery of Subiaco near Rome by Sweynheym and Pannartz, with a rather compressed type, which appears in only three known books. He at once designed a lower case alphabet on this model, but was not satisfied with it and did not have it cut. This was his last actual experiment in the designing of type, though he sometimes talked of designing a new fount, and of having the Golden type cut in a larger size.

NEXT in importance to the type are the initials, borders, and ornaments designed by William Morris. The first book contains a single recto border and twenty different initials. In the next book, Poems by the Way, the number of different initials is fifty-nine. These early initials, many of which were soon discarded, are for the most part suggestive, like the first border, of the ornament in Italian manuscripts of the fifteenth century. In Blunt's Love Lyrics there are seven letters of a new alphabet, with backgrounds of naturalesque grapes and vine leaves, the result of a visit to Beauvais, where the great porches are carved with vines, in August, 1891. From that time onwards fresh designs were constantly added, the tendency being always towards larger foliage and lighter backgrounds, as the early initials were found to be sometimes too dark for the type. The total number of initials of various sizes designed for the Kelmscott Press, including a few that were engraved but never used, is three hundred and eighty-four. Of the letter T alone there are no less than thirty-four varieties.

THE total number of different borders engraved for the Press, including one that was not used, but excluding the three borders designed for The Earthly Paradise by R. Catterson-Smith, is fifty-seven. The first book to contain a marginal ornament, other than these full borders, was The Defence of Guenevere, which has a half-border on p. 74. There are two others in the preface to The Golden Legend. The Recuyell of the Historyes of Troye is the first book in which there is a profusion of such ornament. One hundred and eight different designs for marginal ornaments were engraved. Besides the above-named designs, there are seven frames for the pictures in The Glittering Plain, one frame for those in a projected edition of The House of the Wolfings, nineteen frames for the pictures in the Chaucer (one of which was not used in the book), twenty-eight title-pages and inscriptions, twenty-six large initial words for the Chaucer, seven initial words for The Well at the World's End and The Water of the Wondrous Isles, four line-endings, and three printer's marks, making a total of six hundred and forty-four designs by William Morris, drawn and engraved within seven years. All the initials and ornaments that recur were printed from electrotypes, while most of the title-pages and initial words were printed direct from the wood. The illustrations by Sir Edward Burne-Jones, Walter Crane, and C. M. Gere were also, with one or two exceptions, printed from the wood. The original designs by Sir E. Burne-Jones were nearly all in pencil, and were redrawn in ink by R. Catterson-Smith, and in a few cases by C. Fairfax Murray; they were then revised by the artist and transferred to the wood by means of photography. The twelve designs by A. J. Gaskin for Spenser's Shepheardes Calender, the map in The Sundering Flood, and the thirty-five reproductions in Some German Woodcuts of the Fifteenth Century, were printed from process blocks.

ALL the wood blocks for initials, ornaments, and illustrations, were engraved by W. H. Hooper, C. E. Keates, and W. Spielmeyer, except the twenty-three blocks for The Glittering Plain, which were engraved by A. Leverett, and a few of the earliest initials, engraved by G. F. Campfield. The whole of these wood blocks have been sent to the British Museum, and have been accepted with a condition that they shall not be reproduced or printed from for the space of a hundred years. The electrotypes have been destroyed. In taking this course, which was sanctioned by William Morris when the matter was talked of shortly before his death, the aim of the trustees has been to keep the series of Kelmscott Press books as a thing apart, and to prevent the designs becoming stale by constant repetition. Many of them have been stolen and parodied in America, but in this country they are fortunately copyright. The type remains in the hands of the trustees, and will be used for the printing of its designer's works, should special editions be called for. Other books of which he would have approved may also be printed with it; the absence of initials and ornament will always distinguish them sufficiently from the books printed at the Kelmscott Press.

THE nature of the English hand-made paper used at the Press has been described by William Morris in the foregoing article. It was at first supplied in sheets of which the dimensions were sixteen inches by eleven. Each sheet had as a watermark a conventional primrose between the initials W. M. As stated above, The Golden Legend was to have been the first book put in hand, but as only two pages could have been printed at a time, and this would have made it very costly, paper of double the size was ordered for this work, and The Story of the Glittering Plain was begun instead. This book is a small quarto, as are its five immediate successors, each sheet being folded twice. The last ream of the smaller size of paper was used on The Order of Chivalry. All the other volumes of that series are printed in octavo, on paper of the double size. For the Chaucer a stouter and slightly larger paper was needed. This has for its watermark a Perch with a spray in its mouth. Many of the large quarto books were printed on this paper, of which the first two reams were delivered in February, 1893. Only one other size of paper was used at the Kelmscott Press. The watermark of this is an Apple, with the initials W. M., as in the other two watermarks. The books printed on this paper are The Earthly Paradise, The Floure and the Leafe, The Shepheardes Calender, and Sigurd the Volsung. The last-named is a folio, and the open book shows the size of the sheet, which is about eighteen inches by thirteen. The first supply of this Apple paper was delivered on March 15, 1895.

EXCEPT in the case of Blunt's Love Lyrics, The Nature of Gothic, Biblia Innocentium, The Golden Legend, and The Book of Wisdom and Lies, a few copies of all the books were printed on vellum. The six copies of The Glittering Plain were printed on very fine vellum obtained from Rome, of which it was impossible to get a second supply as it was all required by the Vatican. The vellum for the other books, except for two or three copies of Poems by the Way, which were on the Roman vellum, was supplied by H. Band of Brentford, and by W. J. Turney & Co. of Stourbridge. There are three complete vellum sets in existence, and the extreme difficulty of completing a set after the copies are scattered, makes it unlikely that there will ever be a fourth.

THE black ink which proved most satisfactory, after that of more than one English firm had been tried, was obtained from Hanover. William Morris often spoke of making his own ink, in order to be certain of the ingredients, but his intention was never carried out.

THE binding of the books in vellum and in half-holland was from the first done by J. & J. Leighton. Most of the vellum used was white, or nearly so, but William Morris himself preferred it dark, and the skins showing brown hair-marks were reserved for the binding of his own copies of the books. The silk ties of four colours, red, blue, yellow, and green, were specially woven and dyed.

IN the following section fifty-two works, in sixty-six volumes, are described as having been printed at the Kelmscott Press, besides the two pages of Froissart's Chronicles. It is scarcely necessary to add that only hand presses have been used, of the type known as 'Albion.' In the early days there was only one press on which the books were printed, besides a small press for taking proofs. At the end of May, 1891, larger premises were taken at 14, Upper Mall, next door to the cottage already referred to, which was given up in June.

IN November, 1891, a second press was bought, as The
Golden Legend was not yet half finished, and it seemed as
though the last of its 1286 pages would never be reached.
Three years later another small house was taken, No. 14
being still retained. This was No. 21, Upper Mall, overlooking the river, which acted as a reflector, so that there
was an excellent light for printing. In January, 1895, a
third press, specially made for the work, was set up here
in order that two presses might be employed on the Chaucer. This press has already passed into other hands, and
the little house, with its many associations, and its pleasant outlook towards Chiswick and Mortlake, is now being
transformed into a granary. The last sheet printed there
was that on which are the frontispiece and title of this book.

14, UPPER MALL, HAMMERSMITH, JANUARY 4, 1898.

THE IDEAL BOOK: AN ADDRESS BY
WILLIAM MORRIS, DELIVERED BEFORE
THE BIBLIOGRAPHICAL SOCIETY OF
LONDON, MDCCCXCIII.

Y the Ideal Book, I suppose we are to understand a book not limited by commercial exigencies of price: we can do what we like with it, according to what its nature, as a book, demands of art. But we may conclude, I think, that its matter will limit us somewhat; a work on differential calculus, a medical work, a dictionary, a collection of a statesman's speeches, or a treatise on manures, such books, though they might be handsomely and well printed, would scarcely receive ornament with the same exuberance as a volume of lyrical poems, or a standard classic, or such like.

A work on Art, I think, bears less of ornament than any other kind of book ("non bis in idem" is a good motto); again, a book that must have illustrations, more or less utilitarian, should, I think, have no actual ornament at all, because the ornament and the illustration must almost certainly fight.

STILL whatever the subject matter of the book may be, and however bare it may be of decoration, it can still be a work of art, if the type be good and attention be paid to its general arrangement. All here present, I should suppose, will agree in thinking an opening of Schœffer's 1462 Bible beautiful, even when it has neither been illuminated nor rubricated; the same may be said of Schussler, or Jenson, or, in short, of any of the good old printers; their books, without any further ornament than they derived from the design and arrangement of the letters, were definite works of art.

IN fact a book, printed or written, has a tendency to be a beautiful object, and that we of this age should generally produce ugly books, shows, I fear, something like malice prepense—a determination to put our eyes in our pockets wherever we can.

WELL, I lay it down, first, that a book quite unornamented can look actually and positively beautiful, and not merely un-ugly, if it be, so to say, architecturally good, which, by the by, need not add much to its price, since it costs no more to pick up pretty stamps than ugly ones, and the taste and forethought that goes to the proper setting, position, and so on, will soon grow into a habit, if cultivated, and will not take up much of the master printer's time when taken with his other necessary business.

NOW, then, let us see what this architectural arrangement claims of us. First, the pages must be clear and easy to read; which they can hardly be unless, Secondly, the type is well designed; and Thirdly, whether the margins be small or big, they must be in due proportion to the page of the letter.

FOR clearness of reading the things necessary to be heeded are, first, that the letters should be properly put on their bodies, and, I think, especially that there should be small whites between them; it is curious, but to me certain, that the irregularity of some early type, notably the roman letter of the early printers of Rome, which is, of all roman type, the rudest, does not tend toward illegibility: what does so is the lateral compression of the letter, which necessarily involves the over thinning out of its shape. Of course I do not mean to say that the above-mentioned irregularity is other than a fault to be corrected. One thing should never be done in ideal printing, the spacing out of letters—that is, putting an extra white between them; except in such hurried and unimportant work as newspaper printing, it is inexcusable.

THIS leads to the second matter on this head, the lateral spacing of words (the whites between them); to make a beautiful page great attention should be paid to this, which, I fear, is not often done. No more white should be used between the words than just clearly cuts them off from one another; if the whites are bigger than this it both tends to illegibility and makes the page ugly. I remember once buying a handsome fifteenth-century Venetian book, and I could not tell at first why some of its pages were so worrying to read, and so commonplace and vulgar to look at, for there was no fault to find with the type. But presently it was accounted for by the spacing: for the said pages were spaced like a modern book, i. e., the black and white nearly equal.

NEXT, if you want a legible book, the white should be clear and the black black. When that excellent journal, the Westminster Gazette, first came out, there was a discussion on the advantages of its green paper, in which a good deal of nonsense was talked. My friend, Mr. Jacobi, being a practical printer, set these wise men right, if they noticed his letter, as I fear they did not, by pointing out that what they had done was to lower the tone (not the moral tone) of the paper, and that, therefore, in order to make it as legible as ordinary black and white, they should make their black blacker—which of course they do not do. You may depend upon it that a grey page is very trying to the eyes.

AS above said, legibility depends also much on the design of the letter: and again I take up the cudgels against compressed type, and that especially in roman letter: the full-sized lower-case letters "a," "b," "d," and "c," should be designed

on something like a square to get good results: otherwise one
may fairly say that there is no room for the design; further-
more, each letter should have its due characteristic drawing,
the thickening out for a "b," "e," "g," should not be of the
same kind as that for a "d"; a "u" should not merely be an
"n" turned upside down; the dot of the "i" should not be a cir-
cle drawn with compasses; but a delicately drawn diamond,
and so on. To be short, the letters should be designed by
an artist, and not an engineer. As to the forms of letters in
England (I mean Great Britain), there has been much prog-
ress within the last forty years. The sweltering hideousness
of the Bodoni letter, the most illegible type that was ever
cut, with its preposterous thicks and thins, has been mostly
relegated to works that do not profess anything but the bald-
est utilitarianism (though why even utilitarianism should
use illegible types, I fail to see), and Caslon's letter and the
somewhat wiry, but in its way, elegant old-faced type cut
in our own days, has largely taken its place. It is rather
unlucky, however, that a somewhat low standard of excellence has been accepted for the design of modern roman type
at its best, the comparatively poor and wiry letter of Plantin
and the Elzevirs having served for the model, rather than
the generous and logical designs of the fifteenth-century
Venetian printers, at the head of whom stands Nicholas Jenson; when it is so obvious that this is the best and clearest
roman type yet struck, it seems a pity that we should make
our starting-point for a possible new departure at any period
worse than the best. If any of you doubt the superiority of
this type over that of the seventeenth century, the study
of a specimen enlarged about five times will convince him,
I should think. I must admit, however, that a commercial
consideration comes in here, to wit, that the Jenson letters
take up more room than the imitations of the seventeenth
century; and that touches on another commercial difficulty,
to wit, that you cannot have a book either handsome or clear
to read which is printed in small characters. For my part,
except where books smaller than an ordinary octavo are
wanted, I would fight against anything smaller than pica;

but at any rate small pica seems to me the smallest type that should be used in the body of any book. I might suggest to printers that if they want to get more in they can reduce the size of the leads, or leave them out altogether. Of course this is more desirable in some types than in others; Caslon's letter, e. g., which has long ascenders and descenders, never needs leading, except for special purposes.

I have hitherto had a fine and generous roman type in my mind, but after all a certain amount of variety is desirable, and when you have gotten your roman letter as good as the best that has been, I do not think you will find much scope for development of it; I would therefore put in a word for some form of gothic letter for use in our improved printed book. This may startle some of you, but you must remember that except for a very remarkable type used very seldom by Berthelette (I have only seen two books in this type. Bartholomew, the Englishman, and the Gower, of 1532), English black-letter, since the days of Wynkin de Worde, has been always the letter which was introduced from Holland about that time (I except again, of course, the modern imitations of Caxton). Now this, though a handsome and stately letter, is not very easy reading; it is too much compressed, too spiky, and so to say, too prepensely gothic. But there are many types which are of a transitional character and of all degrees of transition, from those which do little more than take in just a little of the crisp floweriness of the gothic, like some of the Mentelin or quasi-Mentelin ones (which, indeed, are models of beautiful simplicity), or say like the letter of the Ulm Ptolemy, of which it is difficult to say whether it is gothic or roman, to the splendid Mainz type, of which, I suppose, the finest specimen is the Schœffer Bible of 1462, which is almost wholly gothic.

THIS gives us a wide field for variety, I think, so I make the suggestion to you, and leave this part of the subject with two remarks: first, that a good deal of the difficulty of reading gothic books is caused by the numerous contractions in them, which were a survival of the practice of the scribes; and in a lesser degree by the over-abundance of tied letters, both of which drawbacks, I take it for granted, would be absent in modern types founded on these semi-gothic letters. And, secondly, that in my opinion the capitals are the strong side of roman and the lower-case of gothic letter, which is but natural, since the roman was originally an alphabet of capitals, and the lower case a gradual deduction from them.

WE now come to the position of the page of print on the paper, which is a most important point, and one that till quite lately has been wholly misunderstood by modern, and seldom done wrong by ancient printers, or indeed by producers of books of any kind. On this head I must begin by reminding you that we only occasionally see one page of a book at a time; the two pages making an opening are really the unit of the book, and this was thoroughly understood by the old book producers. I think you will seldom find a book produced before the eighteenth century, and which has not been cut down by that enemy of books (and of the human race), the binder, in which this rule is not adhered to: that the binder edge (that which is bound in) must be the smallest member of the margins, the head margin must be larger than this, the fore larger still, and the tail largest of all. I assert that, to the eye of any man who knows what proportion is, this looks satisfactory, and that no other does so look.

BUT the modern printer, as a rule, dumps down the page in what he calls the middle of the paper, which is often not even really the middle, as he measures his page from the head line, if he has one, though it is not really a part of the page, but a spray of type only faintly staining the head of the paper. Now I go so far as to say that any book in which the page is properly put on the paper is tolerable to look at, however poor the type may be (always so long as there is no "ornament" which may spoil the whole thing), whereas any book in which the page is wrongly set on the paper is intolerable to look at, however good the type and ornaments may be. I have got on my shelves now a Jenson's Latin Pliny, which, in spite of its beautiful type and handsome painted ornaments, I dare scarcely look at, because the binder (adjectives fail me here) has chopped off two-thirds of the tail margin: such stupidities are like a man with his coat buttoned up behind, or a lady with her bonnet on hind-side foremost.

BEFORE I finish I should like to say a word concerning large-paper copies. I am clean against them, though I have sinned a good deal in that way myself, but that was in the days of ignorance, and I petition for pardon on that ground only. If you want to publish a handsome edition of a book, as well as a cheap one, do so, but let them be two books, and if you (or the public) cannot afford this, spend your ingenuity and your money in making the cheap book as sightly as you can. Your making a large-paper copy out of the small one lands you in a dilemma even if you re-impose the pages for the large paper, which is not often done, I think. If the margins are right for the smaller book they must be wrong for the larger, and you have to offer the public the worse book at the bigger price; if they are right for the large paper they are wrong for the small, and thus spoil it, as we have seen above that they must do; and that seems scarcely fair to the general public (from the point of view of artistic morality) who might have had a book that was sightly, though not high-priced.

AS to the paper of our ideal book, we are at a great disadvantage compared with past times. Up to the end of the fifteenth, or indeed, the first quarter of the sixteenth centuries, no bad paper was made, and the greater part was very good indeed. At present there is very little good paper made and most of it is very bad. Our ideal book must, I think, be printed on hand-made paper as good as it can be made; penury here will make a poor book of it. Yet if machine-made paper must be used, it should not profess fineness or luxury, but should show itself for what it is: for my part I decidedly prefer the cheaper papers that are used for the journals, so far as appearance is concerned, to the thick, smooth, sham-fine papers on which respectable books are printed, and the worst of these are those which imitate the structure of hand-made papers.

BUT, granted your hand-made paper, there is something to be said about the substance. A small book should not be printed on thick paper, however good it may be. You want a book to turn over easily, and to lie quiet while you are read-ing it, which is impossible, unless you keep heavy paper for big books.

AND, by the way, I wish to make a protest against the super-stition that only small books are comfortable to read; some small books are tolerably comfortable, but the best of them are not so comfortable as a fairly big folio, the size, say, of an uncut Polyphilus or somewhat bigger. The fact is, a small book seldom does lie quiet, and you have to cramp your hand by holding it or else put it on the table with a parapher-nalia of matters to keep it down, a tablespoon on one side, a knife on another, and so on, which things always tumble off at a critical moment, and fidget you out of the repose which is absolutely necessary to reading; whereas, a big folio lies quiet and majestic on the table, waiting kindly till you please to come to it, with its leaves flat and peaceful, giving you no trouble of body, so that your mind is free to enjoy the literature which its beauty enshrines.

SO far then, I have been speaking of books whose only orna-ment is the necessary and essential beauty which arises out of the fitness of a piece of craftsmanship for the use which it is made for. But if we get as far as that, no doubt from such craftsmanship definite ornament will arise, and will be used, sometimes with wise forbearance, sometimes with prodigality equally wise. Meantime, if we really feel impelled to ornament our books, no doubt we ought to try what we can do; but in this attempt we must remember one thing, that if we think the ornament is ornamentally a part of the book merely because it is printed with it, and bound up with it, we shall be much mistaken. The ornament must form as much a part of the book as the type itself, or it will miss its mark, and in order to succeed, and to be ornament, it must submit to certain limitations, and become architectural; a mere black and white picture, however interesting it may be as a picture, may be far from an ornament in a book; while on the other hand a book ornamented with pictures that are suitable for that, and that alone, may become a work of art second to none, save a fine building duly decorated, or a fine piece of literature.

THESE two latter things are, indeed, the one absolutely necessary gift that we should claim of art. The picture-book is not, perhaps, absolutely necessary to man's life, but it gives us such endless pleasure, and is so intimately connected with the other absolutely necessary art of imaginative literature that it must remain one of the very worthiest things toward the production of which reasonable men should strive.

Ornaments designed and engraved for Love is Enough.

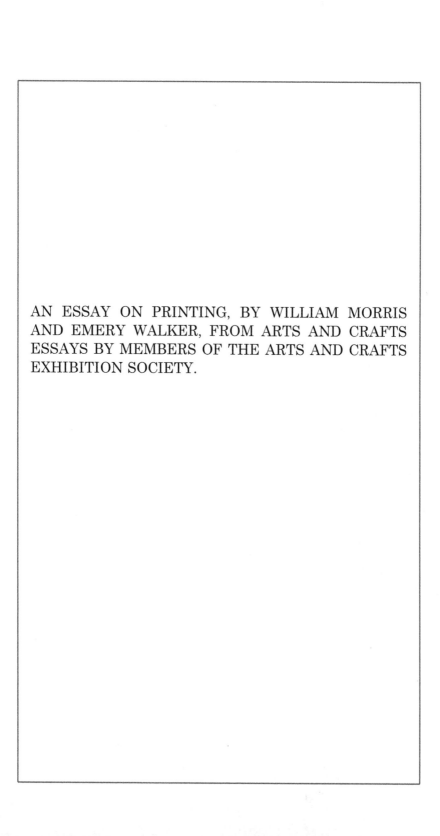

AN ESSAY ON PRINTING, BY WILLIAM MORRIS
AND EMERY WALKER, FROM ARTS AND CRAFTS
ESSAYS BY MEMBERS OF THE ARTS AND CRAFTS
EXHIBITION SOCIETY.

RINTING, in the only sense with which we are at present concerned, differs from most if not from all the arts and crafts represented in the exhibition in being comparatively modern. For although the Chinese took impressions from wood blocks engraved in relief for centuries before the wood-cutters of the Netherlands, by a similar process, produced the block books, which were the immediate predecessors of the true printed book, the invention of movable metal letters in the middle of the fifteenth century may justly be considered as the invention of the art of printing. And it is worth mention in passing that, as an example of fine typography, the earliest book printed with movable types, the Gutenberg, or "forty-two line Bible" of about 1455, has never been surpassed.

PRINTING, then, for our purpose, may be considered as the art of making books by means of movable types. Now, as all books not primarily intended as picture-books consist principally of types composed to form letterpress, it is of the first importance that the letter used should be fine in form; especially as no more time is occupied, or cost incurred, in casting, setting, or printing beautiful letters than in the same operations with ugly ones. And it was a matter of course that in the Middle Ages, when the craftsmen took care that beautiful form should always be a part of their productions whatever they were, the forms of printed letters should be beautiful, and that their arrangement on the page should be reasonable and a help to the shapeliness of the letters themselves. The Middle Ages brought caligraphy to perfection, and it was natural therefore that the forms of printed letters should follow more or less closely those of the written character, and they followed them very closely. The first books were printed in black letter, i. e., the letter which was a Gothic development of the ancient Roman character, and which developed more completely and satisfactorily on the side of the "lower-case" than the capital letters; the "lower-case" being in fact invented in the early Middle Ages.

THE earliest book printed with movable type, the aforesaid Gutenberg Bible, is printed in letters which are an exact imitation of the more formal ecclesiastical writing which obtained at that time; this has since been called "missal type," and was in fact the kind of letter used in the many splendid missals, psalters, etc., produced by printing in the fifteenth century. But the first Bible actually dated (which also was printed at Mainz by Peter Schœffer in the year 1462) imitates a much freer hand, simpler, rounder, and less spiky, and therefore far pleasanter and easier to read. On the whole the type of this book may be considered the ne-plus-ultra of Gothic type, especially as regards the lower-case letters; and type very similar was used during the next fifteen or twenty years not only by Schœffer, but by printers in Strasburg, Basle, Paris, Lubeck, and other cities.

BUT though on the whole, except in Italy, Gothic letter was most often used, a very few years saw the birth of Roman character not only in Italy, but in Germany and France. In 1465 Sweynheim and Pannartz began printing in the monastery of Subiaco near Rome, and used an exceedingly beautiful type, which is indeed to look at a transition between Gothic and Roman, but which must certainly have come from the study of the twelfth or even the eleventh century MSS. They

printed very few books in this type, three only; but in their
very first books in Rome, beginning with the year 1468, they
discarded this for a more completely Roman and far less beautiful letter. But about the same year Mentelin at Strasburg
began to print in a type which is distinctly Roman; and the
next year Gunther Zeiner at Augsburg followed suit; while in
1470 at Paris Udalric Gering and his associates turned out
the first books printed in France, also in Roman character.
The Roman type of all these printers is similar in character,
and is very simple and legible, and unaffectedly designed for
use; but it is by no means without beauty. It must be said
that it is in no way like the transition type of Subiaco, and
though more Roman than that, yet scarcely more like the
complete Roman type of the earliest printers of Rome.

A further development of the Roman letter took place at
Venice. John of Spires and his brother Vindelin, followed
by Nicholas Jenson, began to print in that city, 1469, 1470;
their type is on the lines of the German and French rather
than of the Roman printers. Of Jenson it must be said that
he carried the development of Roman type as far as it can
go: his letter is admirably clear and regular, but at least as
beautiful as any other Roman type. After his death in the
"fourteen eighties," or at least by 1490, printing in Venice
had declined very much; and though the famous family of
Aldus restored its technical excellence, rejecting battered letters, and paying great attention to the "press work" or actual
process of printing, yet their type is artistically on a much
lower level than Jenson's, and in fact they must be considered to have ended the age of fine printing in Italy.

JENSON, however, had many contemporaries who used
beautiful type, some of which—as, e. g., that of Jacobus
Rubeus or Jacques le Rouge—is scarcely distinguishable
from his. It was these great Venetian printers, together with
their brethren of Rome, Milan, Parma, and one or two other
cities, who produced the splendid editions of the Classics,
which are one of the great glories of the printer's art, and

are worthy representatives of the eager enthusiasm for the revived learning of that epoch.

BY far the greater part of these Italian printers, it should be mentioned, were Germans or Frenchmen, working under the influence of Italian opinion and aims. It must be understood that through the whole of the fifteenth and the first quarter of the sixteenth centuries the Roman letter was used side by side with the Gothic. Even in Italy most of the theological and law books were printed in Gothic letter, which was generally more formally Gothic than the printing of the German workmen, many of whose types, indeed, like that of the Subiaco works, are of a transitional character. This was notably the case with the early works printed at Ulm, and in a somewhat lesser degree at Augsburg. In fact Gunther Zeiner's first type (afterwards used by Schussler) is remarkably like the type of the before-mentioned Subiaco books.

IN the Low Countries and Cologne, which were very fertile of printed books, Gothic was the favourite. The characteristic Dutch type, as represented by the excellent printer Gerard Leew, is very pronounced and uncompromising Gothic. This type was introduced into England by Wynkyn de Worde, Caxton's successor, and was used there with very little variation all through the sixteenth and seventeenth centuries, and indeed into the eighteenth. Most of Caxton's own types are of an earlier character, though they also much resemble Flemish or Cologne letter. After the end of the fifteenth century the degradation of printing, especially in Germany and Italy, went on apace; and by the end of the sixteenth century there was no really beautiful printing done: the best, mostly French or Low-Country, was neat and clear, but without any distinction; the worst, which perhaps was the English, was a terrible falling-off from the work of the earlier presses; and things got worse and worse through the whole of the seventeenth century, so that in the eighteenth printing was very miserably performed. In England about this time, an attempt was made (notably by Caslon, who started business in London as a type-founder in 1720) to improve the letter in form. Caslon's type is clear and neat, and fairly well designed; he seems to have taken the letter of the Elzevirs of the seventeenth century for his model: type cast from his matrices is still in everyday use.

IN spite, however, of his praiseworthy efforts, printing had still one last degradation to undergo. The seventeenth century founts were bad rather negatively than positively. But for the beauty of the earlier work they might have seemed tolerable. It was reserved for the founders of the later eighteenth century to produce letters which are positively ugly, and which, it may be added, are dazzling and unpleasant to the eye owing to the clumsy thickening and vulgar thinning of the lines: for the seventeenth-century letters are at least pure and simple in line. The Italian, Bodoni, and the Frenchman, Didot, were the leaders in this luckless change, though our own Baskerville, who was at work some years before them, went much on the same lines; but his letters,[15] though uninteresting and poor, are not nearly so gross and vulgar as those of either the Italian or the Frenchman.

WITH this change the art of printing touched bottom, so far as fine printing is concerned, though paper did not get to its worst till about 1840. The Chiswick press in 1844 revived Caslon's founts, printing for Messrs. Longman the Diary of Lady Willoughby. This experiment was so far successful that about 1850 Messrs. Miller and Richard of Edinburgh were induced to cut punches for a series of "old style" letters. These and similar founts, cast by the above firm and others, have now come into general use and are obviously a great improvement on the ordinary "modern style" in use in England, which is in fact the Bodoni type a little reduced in ugliness. The design of the letters of this modern "old style" leaves a good deal to be desired, and the whole effect is a little too gray, owing to the thinness of the letters. It must be remembered, however, that most modern printing is done by machinery on soft paper, and not by the hand press, and

these somewhat wiry letters are suitable for the machine
process, which would not do justice to letters of more generous design.

IT is discouraging to note that the improvement of the last
fifty years is almost wholly confined to Great Britain. Here
and there a book is printed in France or Germany with some
pretension to good taste, but the general revival of the old
forms has made no way in those countries. Italy is content-
edly stagnant. America has produced a good many showy
books, the typography, paper, and illustrations of which are,
however, all wrong, oddity rather than rational beauty and
meaning being apparently the thing sought for both in the
letters and the illustrations.

TO say a few words on the principles of design in typography: it is obvious that legibility is the first thing to be aimed
at in the forms of the letters; this is best furthered by the
avoidance of irrational swellings and spiky projections, and
by the using of careful purity of line. Even the Caslon type
when enlarged shows great shortcomings in this respect: the
ends of many of the letters such as the t and e are hooked[16]
up in a vulgar and meaningless way, instead of ending in the
sharp and clear stroke of Jenson's letters; there is a gross-
ness in the upper finishings of letters like the c, the a, and
so on, an ugly pear-shaped swelling defacing the form of the
letter: in short, it happens to this craft, as to others, that the
utilitarian practice, though it professes to avoid ornament,
still clings to a foolish, because misunderstood convention-
ality, deduced from what was once ornament, and is by no
means useful; which title can only be claimed by artistic
practice, whether the art in it be conscious or unconscious.

IN no characters is the contrast between the ugly and vulgar
illegibility of the modern type and the elegance and legibility
of the ancient more striking than in the Arabic numerals. In
the old print each figure has its definite individuality, and
one cannot be mistaken for the other; in reading the modern
figures the eyes must be strained before the reader can have

any reasonable assurance that he has a 5, an 8, or a 3 before him, unless the press work is of the best; this is awkward if you have to read Bradshaw's Guide in a hurry.

ONE of the differences between the fine type and the utilitarian must probably be put down to a misapprehension of a commercial necessity: this is the narrowing of the modern letters. Most of Jenson's letters are designed within a square, the modern letters are narrowed by a third or thereabout; but while this gain of space very much hampers the possibility of beauty of design, it is not a real gain, for the modern printer throws the gain away by putting inordinately wide spaces between his lines, which, probably, the lateral compression of his letters renders necessary. Commercialism again compels the use of type too small in size to be comfortable reading: the size known as "Long primer" ought to be the smallest size used in a book meant to be read. Here, again, if the practice of "leading" were retrenched larger type could be used without enhancing the price of a book.

ONE very important matter in "setting up" for fine printing is the "spacing," that is, the lateral distance of words from one another. In good printing the spaces between[17] the words should be as near as possible equal (it is impossible that they should be quite equal except in lines of poetry); modern printers understand this, but it is only practised in the very best establishments. But another point which they should attend to they almost always disregard; this is the tendency to the formation of ugly meandering white lines or "rivers" in the page, a blemish which can be nearly, though not wholly, avoided by care and forethought, the desirable thing being "the breaking of the line" as in bonding masonry or brickwork, thus:

The general solidity of a page is much to be sought for: modern printers generally overdo the "whites" in the spacing, a defect probably forced on them by the characterless quality of the letters. For where these are boldly and carefully designed, and each letter is thoroughly individual in form, the words may be set much closer together, without loss of clearness. No definite rules, however, except the avoidance of "rivers" and excess of white, can be given for the spacing, which requires the constant exercise of judgment and taste on the part of the printer.

THE position of the page on the paper should be considered if the book is to have a satisfactory look. Here once more the almost invariable modern practice is in opposition to a natural sense of proportion. From the time when books first took their present shape till the end of the sixteenth century, or indeed later, the page so lay on the paper that there was more space allowed to the bottom and fore margin than to the top and back of the paper, thus:

THE unit of the book being looked on as the two pages form-ing an opening. The modern printer, in the teeth of the evidence given by his own eyes, considers the single page as the unit, and prints the page in the middle of his paper[18]— only nominally so, however, in many cases, since when he uses a headline he counts that in, the result as measured by the eye being that the lower margin is less than the top one, and that the whole opening has an upside-down look verti-cally, and that laterally the page looks as if it were being driven off the paper.

THE paper on which the printing is to be done is a neces-sary part of our subject: of this it may be said that though there is some good paper made now, it is never used except for very expensive books, although it would not materially increase the cost in all but the very cheapest. The paper that is used for ordinary books is exceedingly bad even in this country, but is beaten in the race for vileness by that made in America, which is the worst conceivable. There seems to be no reason why ordinary paper should not be bet-ter made, even allowing the necessity for a very low price;

but any improvement must be based on showing openly that the cheap article is cheap, e. g., the cheap paper should not sacrifice toughness and durability to a smooth and white surface, which should be indications of a delicacy of material and manufacture which would of necessity increase its cost. One fruitful source of badness in paper is the habit that publishers have of eking out a thin volume by printing it on thick paper almost of the substance of cardboard, a device which deceives nobody, and makes a book very unpleasant to read. On the whole, a small book should be printed on paper which is as thin as may be without being transparent. The paper used for printing the small highly ornamented French service-books about the beginning of the sixteenth century is a model in this respect, being thin, tough, and opaque. However, the fact must not be blinked that machine-made paper cannot in the nature of things be made of so good a texture as that made by hand.

THE ornamentation of printed books is too wide a subject to be dealt with fully here; but one thing must be said on it. The essential point to be remembered is that the ornament, whatever it is, whether picture or pattern-work, should[19] form part of the page, should be a part of the whole scheme of the book. Simple as this proposition is, it is necessary to be stated, because the modern practice is to disregard the relation between the printing and the ornament altogether, so that if the two are helpful to one another it is a mere matter of accident. The due relation of letter to pictures and other ornament was thoroughly understood by the old printers; so that even when the woodcuts are very rude indeed, the proportions of the page still give pleasure by the sense of richness that the cuts and letter together convey. When, as is most often the case, there is actual beauty in the cuts, the books so ornamented are amongst the most delightful works of art that have ever been produced. Therefore, granted well-designed type, due spacing of the lines and words, and proper position of the page on the paper, all books might be at least comely and well-looking: and if to these good qualities were added really beautiful ornament and pictures, printed books might once again illustrate to the full the position of our Society that a work of utility might be also a work of art, if we cared to make it so.

NOTE TO THE PRESENT EDITION: THE FOLLOWING PAGES SHOWING THE TROY AND CHAUCER TYPES ARE PRINTED FROM PROCESS BLOCKS TO INSURE FIDELITY TO THE ORIGINALS. THE FRONTISPIECE AND FIRST PAGE OF TEXT ARE ALSO REPRODUCED IN THE SAME MANNER; PAGE ONE, WITHIN THE BORDER, SHOWING THE GOLDEN TYPE, THE ONLY OTHER TYPE USED BY WILLIAM MORRIS.

This is the Troy type

The following passages are given to show the Troy & Chaucer types, and four initials that were designed for the froissart, but never used. THE land is a little land, Sirs, too much shut up within the narrow seas, as it seems, to have much space for swelling into hugeness: there are no great wastes overwhelming in their dreariness, no great solitudes of forests, no terrible untrodden mountain/walls: all is measured, mingled, varied, gliding easily one thing into another: little rivers, little plains, swelling, speed-ily/changing uplands, all beset with handsome orderly trees; little hills, little mountains, netted over with the walls of sheep/walks: all is little; yet not foolish and blank, but serious rather, and abundant of meaning for

HE following passages are given to show the Troy & Chaucer types, and four initials that were designed for the Froissart, but never used. The land is a little land, Sirs, too much shut up within the narrow seas, as it seems, to have much space for swelling into hugeness: there are no great wastes overwhelming in their dreariness, no great solitudes of forests, no terrible untrodden mountain-walls: all is measured, mingled, varied, gliding easily one thing into another: little rivers, little plains, swelling, speed-ily-changing uplands, all beset with handsome orderly trees; little hills, little mountains, netted over with the walls of sheep-walks: all is little; yet not foolish and blank, but seri-ous rather, and abundant of meaning for such as choose to seek it: it is neither prison, nor palace, but a decent home.

such as choose to seek it: it is neither prison, nor palace, but a decent home.

ALL WHICH I NEITHER praise nor blame, but say that so it is: some people praise this homeliness overmuch, as if the land were the very axle-tree of the world; so do not I, nor any unblinded by pride in themselves and all that belongs to them: others there are who scorn it and the tameness of it: not I any the more: though it would indeed be hard if there were nothing else in the world, no wonders, no terrors, no unspeakable beauties. Yet when we think what a small part of the world's history, past, present, & to come, is this land we live in, and how much smaller still in the history of the arts, & yet how our forefathers clung to it, and with what care and

This is the Troy type

ALL which I neither praise nor blame, but say that so it is: some people praise this homeliness overmuch, as if the land were the very axle-tree of the world; so do not I, nor any unblinded by pride in themselves and all that belongs to them: others there are who scorn it and the tameness of it: not I any the more: though it would indeed be hard if there were nothing else in the world, no wonders, no terrors, no unspeakable beauties. Yet when we think what a small part of the world's history, past, present, & to come, is this land we live in, and how much smaller still in the history of the arts, & yet how our forefathers clung to it, and with what care and pains they adorned it, this unromantic, uneventful-looking land of England, surely by this too our hearts may be touched and our hope quickened.

pains they adorned it, this unromantic, uneventful-looking land of England, surely by
this too our hearts may be touched and our
hope quickened.

FOR as was the land,
such was the art of it
while folk yet troub-
led themselves about
such things; it strove
little to impress peo-
ple either by pomp or
ingenuity: not unsel-
dom it fell into com-
monplace, rarely it rose
into majesty; yet was it never oppressive, never a slave's nightmare or an
insolent boast: & at its best it had an
inventiveness, an individuality, that
grander styles have never overpassed: its best too, and that was in its
very heart, was given as freely to the
yeoman's house, and the humble village church, as to the lord's palace or
the mighty cathedral: never coarse,
though often rude enough, sweet, natural & unaffected, an art of peasants
rather than of merchant princes or courtiers, it must be a hard heart, I think, that
does not love it: whether a man has been born
among it like ourselves, or has come wonder-

FOR as was the land, such was the art of
it while folk yet troubled themselves about
such things; it strove little to impress people
either by pomp or ingenuity: not unseldom
it fell into commonplace, rarely it rose into
majesty; yet was it never oppressive, never
a slave's nightmare or an insolent boast: & at its best it had
an inventiveness, an individuality, that grander styles have
never overpassed: its best too, and that was in its very heart,
was given as freely to the yeoman's house, and the humble
village church, as to the lord's palace or the mighty cathedral: never coarse, though often rude enough, sweet, natural
& unaffected, an art of peasants rather than of merchant
princes or courtiers, it must be a hard heart, I think, that
does not love it: whether a man has been born among it like
ourselves, or has come wonderingly on its simplicity from all
the grandeur over-seas.

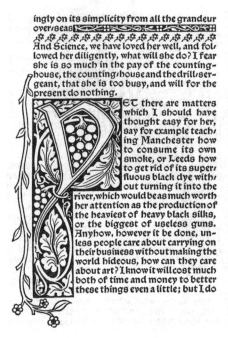

AND Science, we have loved her well, and followed her diligently, what will she do? I fear she is so much in the pay of the counting-house, the counting-house and the drill-sergeant, that she is too busy, and will for the present do nothing.

ET there are matters which I should have thought easy for her, say for example teaching Manchester how to consume its own smoke, or Leeds how to get rid of its superfluous black dye without turning it into the river, which would be as much worth her attention as the production of the heaviest of heavy black silks, or the biggest of useless guns. Anyhow, however it be done, unless people care about carrying on their business without making the world hideous, how can they care about art? I know it will cost much both of time and money to better these things even a little; but I do not see how these can be better spent than in making life cheerful & honourable for others and for ourselves; and the gain of good life to the country at large that would result from men seriously setting about the bettering of the decency of our big towns would be priceless, even if nothing specially good befell the arts in consequence: I do not know that it would; but I should begin to think matters hopeful if men turned their attention to such things, and I repeat that, unless they do so, we can scarcely even begin with any hope our endeavours for the bettering of the Arts. (From the lecture called The Lesser Arts, in Hopes and fears for Art, by William Morris, pages 22 and 33.)

not see how these can be better spent than in making life cheerful & honourable for others and for ourselves; and the gain of good life to the country at large that would result from men seriously setting about the bettering of the decency of our big towns would be priceless, even if nothing specially good befell the arts in consequence: I do not know that it would; but I should begin to think matters hopeful if men turned their attention to such things, and I repeat that, unless they do so, we can scarcely even begin with any hope our endeavours for the bettering of the Arts.

(FROM A LECTURE ENTITLED 'THE LESSER ARTS, IN HOPES AND FEARS FOR ART', BY WILLIAM MORRIS, PAGES 22 AND 33.)

HERE ENDS THE ART AND CRAFT OF PRINTING;
COLLECTED ESSAYS BY WILLIAM MORRIS. OF THIS
BOOK THERE HAVE BEEN PRINTED TWO HUN-
DRED AND TEN COPIES BY CLARKE CONWELL AT
THE ELSTON PRESS: FINISHED THIS THIRTIETH
DAY OF JANUARY MDCCCCII. SOLD BY CLARKE
CONWELL AT THE ELSTON PRESS, PELHAM ROAD,
NEW ROCHELLE, NEW YORK.

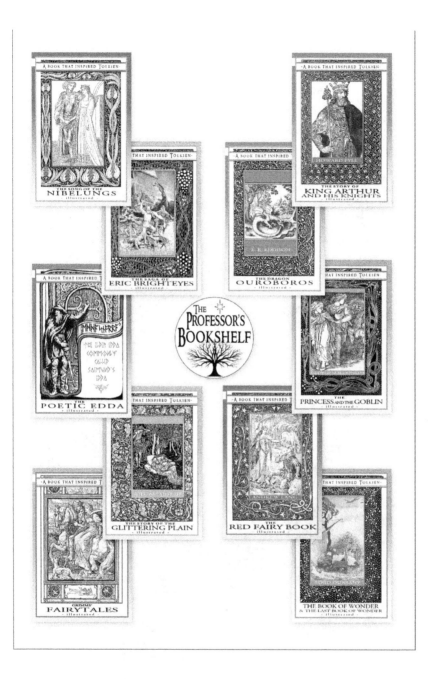

Some titles in The Professor's Bookshelf series

THE ILL-MADE MUTE

CECILIA DART-THORNTON

Cecilia Dart-Thornton

THE ILL-MADE MUTE
Book I of The Bitterbynde Trilogy

The Stormriders land their splendid winged stallions on the airy battlements of Isse Tower. Far below, the superstitious servants who dwell in the fortress' lower depths tell frightening tales of wicked creatures inhabiting the world outside, a world they have only glimpsed. Yet it is the least of the lowly, a mute, scarred, and utterly despised foundling, who dares to scale the Tower, stow away aboard a Windship, and then dive from the sky.

The fugitive is rescued by a kind-hearted adventurer, who bestows a name, the gift of communicating by handspeak, and an amazing truth never before guessed. Now the foundling begins a journey to distant Caermelor, to seek a wise woman whose skills may prove life-changing.

Along the way, this shunned outsider with an angel's soul and a gargoyle's face must survive in a wilderness of extraordinary danger. And as the challenges grow more deadly Imrhien learns something more terrifying than all the evil eldritch wights combined . . .

In a thrilling debut combining storytelling mastery with a treasure trove of folklore, Cecilia Dart-Thornton creates an exceptional epic adventure.

'Not since Tolkien's *The Fellowship of the Ring*... have I been so impressed by a beautifully spun fantasy.'
ANDRE NORTON, GRAND MASTER OF SCIENCE FICTION.

THE PROFESSOR'S BOOKSHELF

Stories that inspired Professor Tolkien,
author of 'The Lord of the Rings'

www.professorsbookshelf.com

CPSIA information can be obtained
at www.ICGtesting.com
Printed in the USA
LVHW041946090223
739117LV00009B/924